The GET RICH QUICK CLUB 2

KERCHING!

*For Patrick
and Joshua, Jordan and James – the
original Dangerous Brothers*

ORCHARD BOOKS
338 Euston Road, London NW1 3BH
Orchard Books Australia
Level 17/207 Kent Street, Sydney, NSW 2000

A paperback original
First published in 2012

ISBN 978 1 40831 209 4

Text © Rose Impey 2012
Cover illustrations © Andy Smith 2012
Inside illustrations by Dynamo © Orchard Books 2012

A CIP catalogue record for this book is available
from the British Library.

1 3 5 7 9 10 8 6 4 2

Printed in Great Britain

Orchard Books is a division of Hachette Children's Books,
an Hachette UK company.

Sneaky-Peeky
Crew

Rose Impey

ORCHARD

CHAPTER 1

Nice to see ya, to see ya…blah, blah, blah.
Welcome to The Get Rich Quick Club. The
club everyone wants to join and I mean *everyone*.
Whatever Baxter tells you, the idea was all mine!
Yours truly: Robin Banks. But you can call me
Banksy.

So, if you want the dough, the dosh, the lolly,
the readies, then you, my friend, have come to the
right place. This is where your whole life could
change. Prepare to be minted!

But first, meet the rest of the dream team.

Next to me on my left, my best mate Baxter – survival expert and King of the Trumps. Next to him, his kid brother Sam, (aka Stinky Sam, on account of his animals). There's also Sam's crazy dog, Glenda the Defender. And last, but not least, Dingdong. Her real name's Annabelle. Get it?

In the beginning, having a girl in the club probably wouldn't have got my vote. Not that we had a lot of choice. She is the Baxters' cousin and lives on the farm next door. But Dingdong has turned out to be a real team player. So you see, even I get things wrong – but not often.

And this is GRQC Headquarters, otherwise known as Baxter's shed. I'd show you inside but it'd probably kill you. Seriously! Toxic fumes. We've threatened Sam with extermination if he doesn't clean out a few cages soon.

In the meantime we're using our summer office – da daa!

Let's get started, because I have got another *unbelievable* story for you! Plus lots of great new business tips. So, if you want to be seriously rich – and who doesn't – pull up a pew and pin back your ears.

Business Tip Number One: Wherever you are, whatever you're doing, *always look for the business possibilities.*

It's what I do, and it's probably the main difference between Baxter and me. Take our last business enterprise: secret surveillance. For Baxter, it was just a good excuse to dress up, camp out and spy on people. But, from the get-go, I could see this was a five star, gold-plated, record-breaking money-spinner. Well, I still say it could have been...

It was the first day of the summer holidays. We

were sitting outside the shed, brainstorming. At least we would have been, if I could have got anyone else's attention.

Dingdong was leafing through a girly magazine. Sam was de-fleaing a hedgehog he'd rescued. And Baxter was sitting on the roof of the shed, hidden behind a pair of binoculars.

They aren't even his binoculars. They're Sam's. Sam bought them off eBay with all the money he made out of the queue for the Happy Hair Saloon. That, you may remember, was another epic business idea of mine.

Baxter said he was just borrowing the binoculars. He'd been borrowing them all week! Baxter's ideas on property can be roughly summed up as: what's mine is mine, and what's Sam's is mine because…I'm bigger – which he is, no argument.

"So, any new money-making ideas?" I asked again.

Sam came up with the usual: charging people to see his collection: Sam's Little Shed of Horrors, as Dingdong calls it. As well as his animals, Sam collects cows' eyeballs, sheep's ear clippings, regurgitated owl pellets…pretty much anything disgusting that stinks!

"That might work," Dingdong said, sarcastically, "if we wanted to kill people off."

I agreed. "Any sensible ideas?" I asked.

Dingdong suggested a talent show.

"That might work," I said, equally sarcastically, "if we had any talent between us."

"Speak for yourself," she snapped. "My dance

teacher says one day I could go a long way. "

"To Mars, hopefully," Baxter shouted down from the shed roof.

"On a one-way ticket," I added.

"You two are so not funny," she snapped.

"What about a spot of spying?" Baxter suggested. He had the binoculars trained on the back gardens of two of our neighbours. "We could sell any secrets we discover."

"Who to?" I said.

"The papers, of course. They love that kind of thing."

I couldn't imagine what newspapers might be interested in Old Crumble's secrets, or Birdy's. They're both ancient and pretty boring.

Old Crumble, or Mr Crump, lives next door to me. He used to be a music teacher when my mum was at school. You know, back in the Dark Ages (ha haa). Birdy, Mrs B, lives next door to him. She was a school cook, probably when they still cooked in cauldrons.

"It'd be a lot easier," Baxter complained, "if they didn't have such high hedges. I don't know why they don't cut 'em lower."

"Maybe they don't want people spying on them," I said.

"And selling their secrets to the papers," Dingdong laughed. Baxter didn't even get the joke.

"If you want to spy on someone," she told him, "you could look for whoever's stealing my dad's eggs. He's going ballistic about it."

I sat up suddenly, sniffing money. "Is he offering a reward?"

"Doubt it," she said, "knowing how tight my dad is."

I slumped back in my seat. My motto is: no money, no point.

"Forget it," said Baxter. "Who'd want to spend

their time watching poultry anyway?" He flapped his elbows and clucked like he was about to lay an egg. Seriously, you'd swear it was a chicken.

"Yeah," I agreed with Baxter. "We'd have to be pretty desperate. Anyone for chicken patrol?" I joined in, flapping and clucking.

Dingdong wasn't amused. She pulled that face, which Baxter says makes her look like a constipated camel. I've never seen a constipated camel, but I bet it looks like that.

"Now, this is more interesting," Baxter suddenly said.

"What is?" I asked, climbing up to join him on the roof. I reached for the binoculars.

"Old Crumble's cruising for a bruising," he said, passing them to me, then dropping heavily to the ground.

Old Crumble was at the top of a tall ladder. What made it interesting was: the ladder was wobbling all over the place.

"Quick," Baxter said. "If he falls off we don't want to miss it."

"What about our money-making ideas?" I called after him.

But I should have known they would have to wait. If there was any chance of blood and guts, Baxter wanted a front row seat. I jumped down and set off with the others.

"Hang on, Mr Crump," we shouted. "Don't fall off before we get there."

CHAPTER TWO

It took us maybe a minute to reach Old Crumble's back gate. In that time, to Baxter's disappointment, he'd got the ladder under control and was on his way down. But then Brutus spotted us, and went bananas, and the ladder was soon wobbling all over the place again.

Brutus is Old Crumble's secret deterrent. Mostly, I like dogs, even Glenda the Defender. But Brutus is seriously scary. We've had three different postmen in the last year and if you ask me he's the reason.

Old Crumble insists he's just a bit unpredictable. So we should never go through the gate, in case. And we never do, not even Baxter who's a magnet for trouble. Today, though, with the gate between us, we felt fairly safe.

Brutus is built like a small beer barrel. He hit the gate like a battering ram. We all backed off, and waited for Old Crumble to get down and control him.

"If it isn't the Dangerous Boys," he said.

He always calls us that; it really bugs Dingdong. Girls can be dangerous, she insists. It's true; I'm the first to run for cover when Dingdong gets rattled.

"What're you up to, Mr Crump?" Baxter asked.

"Now what does it look like?" he replied, grumpily. "I'm installing security lights. In case of intruders!"

"You don't need security lights," Baxter said, waving the binoculars about. "We'll keep an eye on the place for you. You know, like Neighbourhood Watch?"

"And how much will that cost me?" Old Crumble asked.

"Cost you?" Baxter asked, surprised.

"It usually costs me when you lot show up."

"It's a free service," Baxter announced, grandly.

Free! I couldn't believe my ears. Business Tip Number Two: Never, *never*, give anything away free.

I gave Baxter a hefty kick. "When Baxter says free," I explained, "he means almost free."

"Guessed as much," Old Crumble said, turning away.

On the other hand, Business Tip Number Three: Never be afraid to negotiate.

"We'd give you our special discount rate!" I called after him. "Why don't I work out some figures and get back to you."

"You do that," Old Crumble said, disappearing into the house. Brutus hung around the gate, menacingly, his stomach grumbling.

"There's something wrong with that dog," Baxter said.

I had to agree; he sounded like a volcano about to erupt.

"Gas," said Sam, as an eye-watering smell came drifting over the gate to reach us. We all coughed and covered our faces.

The smell was rank.

"Respect!" said Baxter, who's an expert on trumps himself.

"It's probably something he's eaten," said Sam.

But right now we had more important things to think about.

"Back to the shed," I said.

Our shiny new security business was starting to take shape in my head. In fact, I was buzzing with it.

It's what Lord Sugar means when he talks about the entrepreneurial spirit. Getting an idea and running with it.

Lord Sugar started like us with absolutely nothing. He went from zero to hero. Who knows, I thought, this could be where it all starts for us!

"First off, we've got to look professional," I told the others.

Baxter nodded enthusiastically. "Oh, yes, uniforms!" he grinned. He was picturing us all in camo gear, swinging through the trees.

But Dingdong soon put him straight. "If you think I'm dressing up like Action Barbie, you can think again."

"It's very important," Baxter said, seriously, keen to impress us with his survival know-how, "that on a stake-out you try to blend in. Merge into the environment. Disappear!"

"Excellent idea," Dingdong told him. "Now, why don't you?"

"Look," I said quickly, before they started one of their epic arguments, "we could at least have matching caps. You know, with a logo on?"

"A logo's good," Baxter conceded. "We could put it on our business cards."

"And our website," I agreed, getting excited.

"Business cards? Website? What planet are you two on?" Dingdong snorted. "And why would we go to all that trouble?"

Sam agreed. "How's this going to make us any money?"

"Old Crumble's just the beginning," I explained. We'll soon get everyone else on board: our parents, neighbours…

"Who knows, I said, "we might discover some real criminals. Catch them in the act, turn them over to the police…"

"Get our pictures in the papers," Baxter added. "On TV!"

"And earn a big fat reward," I continued.

"Think of it," Baxter said, excitedly, "we'll get to stay out all night on guard."

In your dreams, I thought, but I didn't want to burst Baxter's balloon. "Surely your dad'll be up for it," I told Dingdong.

"He might," she said, slowly coming round to the idea. "'Specially if we find his egg thief for him."

Baxter and me grinned, flapping and clucking again.

"Don't even start," Dingdong warned us. "You two are so…"

"Not funny," Baxter clucked, exactly like a chicken talking.

But Dingdong soon got her own back, when it came to deciding on a business name. I suggested Super Security, then Baxter went one better with SuperSonic Security.

"Sounds like we're planning to launch into space," Dingdong told him. "Although given your track record for disasters that's always possible."

"You come up with something better, then," Baxter told her.

"How about Sneaky-Peeky Crew?" she said.

"Good one," Sam said, high-fiving Dingdong.

Sneaky-Peeky! Baxter and me couldn't believe our ears.

"It's pants," Baxter sneered.

"Desperate," I agreed.

"But it's exactly what we'd be doing," she argued. "Sneaking and peeking. I think we should vote on it."

The result was two all – stalemate. And neither of them would budge. So ten minutes later I shrugged, switching my vote just to get things moving.

"Oh, man," Baxter groaned, clutching his head.

So, Sneaky-Peeky Crew was agreed and we all went home to persuade our parents to sign up.

While I waited for my mum to finish work, I did a few sums to see how much money we might make. Suppose we charged...50p an hour. Surely, people would pay that for a bit of peace of mind. From, say...10am till 7pm...seven days a week for the whole summer...

And that was before we caught any criminals and earned shed loads of dough in reward! Oh, we could be looking at a lot of loot. Mega-bucks, here we come!

CHAPTER THREE

In business, as I often tell the others, you have to be prepared for small setbacks. And, sometimes, big fat ones, too. This felt like one of those times. Even my mum had turned us down!

"But this is full-on surveillance we're offering," I told her.

"Why on earth would I need that?" she said. "Honestly, Robin, can't you find something more useful to do with your summer holiday?"

More useful than making money?! I don't

think so. I clearly didn't get my business sense from my mother.

Baxter hit a big No too, but Dingdong's dad hadn't ruled it out. "He says he'll give me extra pocket money," she told us, smugly, "if we find out who's stealing his eggs."

"Big hairy deal," Baxter said, sarcastically. "That'll really make our fortune."

I agreed with Baxter. Why waste our time on brainless chickens when there were serious crimes to prevent? I reminded the others there were still the neighbours to try.

"Starting with that visit I promised Old Crumble," I said. "Baxter can come with me. Dingdong, Sam, try Hippy Mum and the students. And make sure you give them the hard sell..."

"Yeah, yeah," Dingdong cut me off. "Take no prisoners, blah, blah, blah..."

We found Old Crumble cutting his lawn with a pair of nail scissors. No, not really, but Mum says it looks like he does. The minute he spotted us he ducked inside his greenhouse. It's a flashy new one he's had specially built. It's stuffed with tomatoes and cucumbers and prize-winning geraniums, so he probably thought we couldn't see him. But we could.

"Morning, Mr Crump!" we called, really loudly. When he came out I made him an offer he couldn't possibly refuse.

"50p an hour? In your dreams. Forget it," he said. "Why on earth would I want to pay you to watch my place?"

"You've heard about the egg thief?" said Baxter.

"Could be tomatoes and cucumbers next," I warned him.

"Or prize-winning geraniums," Baxter added. "Not to mention all your valuables."

"You'd be getting complete, round-the-clock security," I said. "Twenty-four seven," Baxter added. "Nothing – and nobody – would get past us."

Old Crumble began to look interested. "Nobody?"

"Nobody," we said together.

"OK, I'll pay you 50p…" Yes! We punched the air, "a day…" he went on.

"A day?!" I said, thinking we must have heard him wrong.

"A day," he repeated. Then, dropping his voice

28

to a whisper, he started pointing. "To watch Her Next Door."

"Birdy?" I asked, surprised.

"Shhh," he whispered. "And that animal of hers!"

Birdy and Old Crumble often argue, usually about her cat, Cosmo, or his dog, Brutus.

He told this rambling story about how Cosmo's always going into his garden and using it as a toilet. Then, when Brutus quite reasonably chases the cat off, Birdy has the cheek to complain about the dog's barking. But Old Crumble's biggest complaint was about Birdy feeding Brutus lumps of bread.

"Why would she do that?" I asked, unconvinced.

"Sabotage," Old Crumble whispered. Baxter and me looked at him like he was one sandwich short of a picnic. "And there's your evidence," he said, pointing towards the dog.

Again we heard that low, gurgling, something-seriously-wrong-with-the-plumbing sound. Then another poisonous, eye-watering trump followed it.

I didn't even know bread's bad for dogs. Sam told us later it's because it ferments in their

stomachs and fills them with gas. Result: Brutus blows up like a balloon and trumps like a machine – even worse than Baxter!

"So, 50p a day is my final offer," Old Crumble told us.

It wasn't the offer we'd been looking for – nothing like it.

"50p *each* a day?" I asked, hopefully.

"Between you," he said, in a voice that made it clear this was his final final offer. "But, if you catch her in the act, there could be a bonus payment."

I sighed and put out my hand to seal the deal. Old Crumble shook it with his mucky gardening hand.

Still, looking on the positive side, we'd got our first customer. The Sneaky-Peeky Crew was in business!

Five minutes later, when Old Crumble went out to walk Brutus, we slipped next door to Birdy's.

"We're starting a new business," we told her. "It's called Sneaky-Peeky Crew."

"That's nice," she said. "Is it something to do with sailing?"

"No," said Baxter. "We watch your house, in case of burglars."

"Like Neighbourhood Watch," I said, cutting to the chase. "We wouldn't charge much," I added quickly.

"It's a good job," she said, "I'm a pensioner, you know."

"So's Mr Crump," Baxter pointed out, "and he's signed up."

"Don't mention that name to me," said Birdy. Then she told us her story. In this version she certainly didn't throw bread over his fence. The villains were Old Crumble, and that ugly beast, Brutus. They terrorised her poor, harmless little cat. And (even though Cosmo never pooed in his garden) Old Crumble regularly put dog poo over her fence – in revenge.

So she wasn't too hard to persuade in the end either.

Baxter and me thought Old Crumble and Birdy were both crazy. But if they were prepared to pay us to watch each other why should we complain? Business is business, right?

Even if it wasn't quite the business we'd been imagining.

When we got back to HQ, Dingdong and Sam were already there. "That was a big fat waste of time," she announced. Hippy Mum had told them she was broke. Then she gave them this big lecture about how we ought to trust people...And send good karma into the world, whatever karma is.

"And don't even ask about the students," Dingdong said, rolling her eyes.

That was no big surprise to me. They claim to be penniless, too, but they still buy beer most nights of the week.

"Well, *we* scored a full house," Baxter said, smugly.

While he told the story, I tried not to look too embarrassed.

But Dingdong quickly put the boot in. "So, let's get this right," she said. "We're too busy to catch my dad's egg thief, because we're doing serious surveillance on a cat…and a dog. Hmmm, important stuff. Woof, woof," she added.

"Miaow, miaow," Sam joined in. Those two are so not funny.

Here's another tip: In business, it's important to stay positive and believe in yourself, *especially* when other people put you down.

I hope you're writing all these tips down. They'll be worth a shed load of money, when I'm famous, you know.

CHAPTER FOUR

The next morning our first job was to find a good place to spy from. As Baxter had pointed out, Old Crumble and Birdy both had really tall hedges. To see into their gardens we'd need to be up a tree, at least.

"We need somewhere we can see them, without them seeing us," I told the others.

"Stop right there, Banksy," Baxter cut me off. "This is my area of expertise. Leave this to me. First things first, though…"

He handed us each a camo cap with a pretty

cool badge he'd drawn and stuck on it. The logo was a pair of scary eyes peeping out of the letters SPC, better than Sneaky-Peeky Crew.

I noticed Baxter's cap was brand new. Ours looked like he'd fished them out from under his bed, or behind a radiator.

"If you think that's going anywhere near my head…" Dingdong started up.

"It only wants a shake," Baxter said, sending clouds of dust into the air. "Don't be such a girl!"

Dingdong didn't even bother to point out the fact that she *was* a girl. But she insisted she still wasn't wearing the hat until it had been fully fumigated. She took it off him, held out between two fingertips.

Mine smelled like something had died in it, which knowing the Baxters was perfectly possible. I didn't want to risk being called a girl, though, so I put it on, trying not to breathe in.

Baxter then gave us each a list of things we'd need to collect and put in a rucksack before we set off.

"It's only a reccy," I said, "we're not exactly going on safari."

"If I'm leading this expedition," Baxter said, "I want to be prepared for every emergency."

Always the most serious emergency, in Baxter's view, is running short of food. So everyone had to pack a picnic. Or, in his case, two.

We finally assembled, much later, with so much equipment we could barely carry it between us. It included towels, ropes, blankets, cushions…

"Cushions?" I said. "Are these really necessary?"

As well as all this, Sam insisted on carrying a spare cage. In case we found undiscovered specimens out there.

"Out where?" I said. "We're only going round the village. It's not exactly unchartered territory."

Finally we were ready to start. "Try to remember," I told the others, "this is an undercover operation. We need to keep a low profile."

"Top secret. Hush, hush," Baxter said, in a stage whisper. "Received and understood."

This just made Dingdong howl, like a hyena.

Then Glenda the Defender started barking and turning somersaults with excitement. Nothing stays a secret for long with this team.

We trudged round the perimeter of the tiny village where we live, twice in different directions. It wasn't like we were in any danger of getting lost. But Baxter kept stopping to consult his compass even though we all knew it was broken. He sat on it once and now you can't rely on anything it tells you. A bit like its owner, come to think of it.

At different points Baxter was stung by a wasp, Dingdong was almost bitten by a horse she tried to feed, and I stepped into a rabbit hole, almost twisting my ankle. I wondered how it was that Baxter could even turn a walk round the village into a dangerous expedition.

Finally, *finally*, he came round to my idea that we'd probably find what we were looking for across the stream.

The stream runs between Baxter's garden and Dingdong's farm. On the farm side there's a really steep bank with massive trees. Exactly what we were looking for, as I'd pointed out earlier.

Today the current was running quite fast. Dingdong looked at it and said, "I think I'll go home and get my wellies."

Before I could agree with her, Baxter said, "Wellies! You don't need wellies, you big wuss! Follow me; I'll lead the way."

I could just see what was coming next.

There were a few flattish rocks that made perfect stepping-stones. Or they would have, if they'd been closer together. Baxter seemed to think his legs were longer than everyone else's. Halfway across he discovered his mistake. He came to a stop with his front leg on one rock, his back leg on another. The rocks were wet and slimy and Baxter's legs slowly began to slide in opposite directions.

They stopped just short of the splits.

"Help!" he yelled.

"Oooh, painful," said Dingdong.

"Torture," I agreed, grinning.

Baxter grabbed at thin air then keeled over sideways. He ended up flat on his back in the stream. We all cheered. I'd have paid good money for an action replay.

Baxter rose up grinning, covered in weeds and soaked to the skin. He climbed back out on our side and shook himself all over us like a big dog. After that there was no point trying to stay dry. We all waded into the stream and hurled lumps of wet moss at each other, but mostly at Dingdong.

Later, when we got bored with that game, we climbed out on the other side. We found the biggest tree at the top of the bank and dumped everything underneath it. All the essential equipment we'd carried and would probably never need. But everyone agreed that bringing a picnic was one of Baxter's better ideas.

After we'd finished scoffing we were finally ready to start work. Or I was. Sam had already gone on a bug hunt; Dingdong was lying on a towel with a bottle of sun screen.

Baxter was looking critically at the makeshift camp we'd set up, shaking his head.

"You know what we need?" he said, seriously. "A new HQ!"

"What the Wayne Rooney for?" I almost yelled.

"For when we're on night duty," he said.

Night duty? I wondered again what fantasy universe Baxter was living in. "We are never going to be allowed out overnight," I told him. Like I was explaining to someone with only half a brain.

"But that's when people need security," he said, like he was talking to someone with no brain at all.

I could tell there was no point arguing and I just shrugged.

"Ways and means, Banksy," he said. "Ways and means."

I had no idea what Baxter was talking about. But I had a horrible feeling it probably spelled T-R-O-U-B-L-E.

CHAPTER FIVE

Next morning I was up and out early, but
Baxter still beat me to it. "He's been gone
for hours," his mum said, when I called for
him. "I don't know what he's up to, but all that
hammering's making me nervous."

It made me nervous too, now that I noticed
it. Baxter and hammers are a bad combination.
As I crossed the stream, the banging got even
louder.

"This is supposed to be secret surveillance," I
hissed at him.

"Keep your boxers on," Baxter told me, waving his hammer.

There were random bits of wood leaning against the tree. It looked like he might be planning a bonfire.

"What's going on here?" I asked.

"This is our new HQ," Baxter told me, proudly. "As you can see it's…almost finished."

I could see that a few pieces of wood had been loosely nailed to the tree. It was clearly going to be

a very rough sort of shelter. Beside it was a piece of plastic netting.

I gave it a scornful kick with my trainer. "What's this for?"

"Camouflage," Sam said, proudly. "Baxter's idea."

Baxter smiled, modestly.

"Camouflage!" I yelled. "But it's bright orange! You can probably see that from outer space."

Baxter gave me the pitying look I always get when I point out flaws in his master plan. But Sam was genuinely disappointed. "You should see inside, Banksy, it's mega scary."

When I was finally persuaded to try it out, I had to agree. It was dark…and scary…and cramped! I was glad to get out.

Then Dingdong arrived. "What this?" she said.

"Baxter's new den. You should try it," I told her.

She gave me and the den a pitying look. "Yeah, and pigs might open a bacon factory."

"You'll all be glad to come inside if it rains," Baxter told us.

But so far it was sunny and I was determined to get started. I took the binoculars and climbed the tree. I left Baxter and Sam still working on their masterpiece. Dingdong followed me up the tree, edging me along the branch.

The good news was from there we had a clear view into both Old Crumble's and Birdy's gardens. Finally, at last, surveillance could begin.

One of us took the binoculars, while the other person wrote it all down in a notebook that I'd brought with me specially.

✷ *1100 hours: Old Crumble cuts the grass. Brutus sleeps on the back step.*

✷ *1105 Birdy hangs out the washing. Cosmo sleeps on a garden seat.*

It went on like that for the next hour…and the next…and the one after that. The most exciting thing that happened all morning was when Brutus woke up and scratched himself.

"What's happening now?" I asked Dingdong, irritably.

"Birdy's at her kitchen window," she said. "Could be washing up. Hard to tell, but she's wearing rubber gloves."

"Never mind rubber gloves," I said even more irritably. "What about the cat?"

"Can't see the cat. Oh, now he's back and he's…
curling up and going to sleep."

"Is that it?" I snapped.

"I could make something up, if you like,"
Dingdong offered.

I realise that in any business, even spying, there's
bound to be dull, routine bits. But this was way
beyond dull. At this rate we'd all die of boredom
before we made any dosh.

Baxter joined us, having left Sam to clear up
down below. Within minutes he was complaining.
"This is bor-ing," he said, as if the fact might have
escaped our attention. "I could fall out of this tree
I'm so bored." He yawned. "It's even more boring
than watching Cash in the Attic with my grandma,"
he moaned on. "Boring, boring, boring!"

"Couldn't be more boring than watching
chickens, could it?" Dingdong asked.

"That's it, I'm going for lunch," Baxter said,

disappearing down the tree.

"I'll stick around," I said, nobly.

"Why would you?" Dingdong asked.

"Well, we might miss something vitally important," I said.

"Yeah, like Brutus chewing a bone," Dingdong said, "or Cosmo taking a leak. Better not miss that. See you, sucker."

And she was right. When the others came back the only thing to report was Cosmo pooing in Old Crumble's flowerbed. And Brutus chasing him off and very nearly catching him. Apart from that – a big fat zero.

By the end of the day my eyes were aching, my bum was numb and I was bored out of my skull. So, when I went to collect our measly 50ps and both Old Crumble and Birdy had the nerve to complain, I was pretty fed up.

"How do I know you've not just been skiving off

having a good time all day?" Old Crumble asked.

"Do I look like I've been having a good time?" I said.

"I'll want more results tomorrow," Birdy warned me, opening her purse like it was full of the crown jewels.

The next day was even worse: dog slept, cat slept, dog scratched, cat licked…Could it be any more boring?

The others found better things to do with themselves, sliding down the bank and paddling in the stream. But I stuck it out like an idiot, until even I had to admit the truth. We were never going to get any real money out of those two.

It had been a complete waste of time.

"It could be worse," Baxter said later, trying to cheer me up. "We could be on chicken patrol. Cluck, cluck."

"You know what," I said, miserably, "I think we'd

have been better off." Of course, I made him swear, on pain of death, not to tell Dingdong that.

Suddenly, he said, "Tell you what, let's do it – tonight. You and me. Let's stay out and find the egg thief. We don't have to tell Dingdong. Then, if we catch him, *we* can claim the money."

"You can't tell Sam, then," I pointed out. Sam's like a leaky tap where secrets are concerned. It didn't really feel fair on the others, but it was tempting…

"Anyway," I shook my head. "They'll never let us stay out overnight."

"Leave that to me," he said, like he was Mr Fix-it. "I'll get my people to talk to your people."

I rolled my eyes and thought, I won't hold my breath.

But somehow he did it. Baxter managed to wind both our mums round his little finger – and tie them in a bow. Don't ask me how.

Sometimes I think Baxter has magic powers.

CHAPTER SIX

ere's another important business tip for you: always listen to your instincts. Right now mine were telling me: don't go, Robin, don't go! But did I listen? Even when Mum started grilling me, and I could have wriggled out of it, I didn't.

"So, how big is this den?" she asked.

"Big enough," I mumbled.

"Not big then. I'm surprised you want to be so close to the King of Trumps." The first time I shared a tent with Baxter he trumped all night.

I'd made the mistake of telling my mum. Now she never lets me forget it.

"And how safe is it? What if it falls on your head in the middle of the night?"

"It won't," I said, although I wasn't at all sure about that.

"What if you're cold? What if it rains?"

"Yeah, yeah," I said, "what if the ground opens up and an army of zombies comes after us?"

"In that case you can wake me. Otherwise I don't want to be disturbed in the middle of the night. Understood, Robin?"

I nodded, relieved she didn't want to come and check the den out. If it barely passed my health and safety standards, it would never pass hers.

We waited until it was almost dark then crept silently down to the stream.

"So, what did you tell Sam?" I whispered.

"That I was sleeping at yours," Baxter whispered back

"D'you think he believed you?"

"'Course he believed me!" Baxter snorted. "Sam believes whatever I tell him."

We each had a rucksack. Baxter's was enormous and weighed a ton!

"What the devil have you got in there?" I asked him.

He smiled. "Let's just say I'm prepared for every eventuality."

I hoped he was because all I'd got was a water bottle, a pillow, a torch and a sleeping bag.

Not that we'd be doing much sleeping, I realised. We'd be on duty. That was the point, wasn't it? Like Baxter said, night time was when people needed security, because that's when burglars were out and about. To be honest, I felt pretty nervous at the thought of that. But Baxter looked far from nervous, so I didn't say anything.

When we got to the den he said, "We'll stow our stuff inside first." He crawled under the netting, and through the gap he calls the doorway, dragging his rucksack after him. When I tried to follow I found my way completely blocked. With Baxter and his bag inside there was barely any room left for me. To be honest that suited me. It was a warm night and I'd have been much happier in the open. But Baxter had put a lot of love and hammering into that den; he was determined we were going to use it.

"Come on, there's bags of room in here," he insisted.

I finally squeezed myself into the tiny strip of space he'd left. Then we sat elbow to elbow with our rucksacks on our knees, completely in the dark. That's when I realised the den's other problem. It was built on a slope.

The only way you could sit, never mind sleep, in there was propped against the tree with your feet braced. The moment I relaxed mine I started to slide down the bank.

"Why don't we leave our sleeping bags in here?" I suggested, "and maybe have a bit of a reccy?" I tried not to sound too desperate to get out.

"If you like," Baxter agreed.

We squeezed ourselves out again and I promised myself nothing – short of zombies – would get me back inside.

Then Baxter said some magic words. "Let's have some grub before we get started, shall we?"

"You brought food?" I said, excitedly, which was probably the stupidest question on the planet.

When Baxter unloaded his rucksack I could see why it had weighed a ton. First he took out a frying pan, then a packet of sausages, a box of eggs, half a loaf of bread, a tin of beans… 'They're for breakfast,' he said. Then doughnuts, marshmallows, crisps, gherkins (don't ask) and cans of Coke. "You are the Cat's Bananas," I said, impressed.

"Aren't I just?" Baxter grinned.

We sat outside the den eating marshmallows sandwiched between crisps. This started to feel like Baxter's best idea ever.

"Have you got a camping stove in there as well?" I asked, out of interest.

But Baxter's mouth was so stuffed he just shook his head.

"So how d'you plan to cook this gourmet breakfast?"

"On a fire, of course," he mumbled. "There's plenty of wood about."

"Matches?" I asked, casually.

Baxter hesitated, then shrugged. "A couple of sticks'll do it. When you're used to roughing it in the wild, like I am," he said, casually, "you learn to improvise, you know."

I didn't argue, but I had a feeling we wouldn't be enjoying a cooked breakfast in the woods any time soon.

While we'd been eating it had got quite a bit darker – and much quieter. Apart from the noise of bats flying overhead and a barn owl hooting it was almost silent.

"It's a good job we didn't bring those two scaredy-cats with us," Baxter said. "They'd have been jumping and twitching every time we heard a sound."

I grinned and sort of nodded, but, to be honest, I wasn't feeling all that brave myself by then.

We'd just started on the last two doughnuts when we heard the sharp SNAP! of twigs cracking under foot. I almost jumped out of my skin. The big question on my mind was: whose foot?

We both stopped eating and went very still. There was the sound of someone – or something – being dragged along the ground. It sounded like it might be…a body! Who-or-whatever-it-was

was very close by now. I waited, hardly daring to breathe.

Then I heard something incredible. It was so incredible I stopped feeling nervous for at least a second or two.

Afterwards Baxter told me I'd imagined it. And I guess I must have, because it was too incredible otherwise.

What I thought I heard was a tiny, strangled little voice, coming out of Baxter's mouth, saying, "Mu-mmy!"

CHAPTER SEVEN

Baxter was gripping my arm so tightly it was actually hurting. I tried to prise his fingers off, until I realised he was attempting to drag me towards the den.

I still don't know how we got inside – in the dark – without a sound. But it's surprising what you can do when you're completely terrified.

Inside we squeezed so tightly together I could hear Baxter's breathing. I could feel his heart racing as fast as mine. The sounds were getting closer. I prayed that whatever it was would keep on going and miss us. But it didn't.

Now there was a scrabbling sound outside the den. Something was trying to find its way in!

I was sure it was some kind of animal: a fox or a badger…Maybe something bigger. I began to imagine even scarier things like a wild boar…or escaped puma. Unlikely, I know, but I read about one once that had got away from a zoo.

But then I started to think: what if it's a zombie?

Yes, I know they don't exist, but when you're that scared anything seems possible. Having an active imagination isn't always a good thing.

Finally, when Baxter managed to turn on his torch, it wasn't a wild animal, at all, or a zombie. Although it was the next best thing.

Through the doorway Sam's face grinned stupidly in at us. "Found you," he said, like we'd all been playing hide and seek.

Before Baxter could ask what the Wayne

Rooney he thought he was doing there, another bigger, far bossier head appeared beside his. "So, you thought you could leave us out, did you?" Dingdong said, grinning. "Well, think again."

"Does Mum know you're both here?" Baxter demanded.

Sam nodded happily. "Dingdong talked her round."

"Didn't take long," Dingdong said. "She knew

it was a safer bet than leaving you two out here on your own. You look a bit green. We didn't give you a fright, did we?"

"Pfff, it'd take more than that to frighten us," Baxter blustered.

"A lot more," I said, trying to back him up.

But Dingdong wasn't taken in. To be honest, I wasn't sorry to see them. You know what they say about safety in numbers? And even Sam and Dingdong had to count as numbers, right?

But turning up just then they had sort of spoiled our fun. And we still didn't want Dingdong to know what we were doing.

"We were just going to try to catch Birdy and Old Crumble out," I said. "You know, when they least expect it."

"That's right," Baxter backed me up. "And now we're going to get to work. You two can finish the picnic," he said, generously.

"Two half-eaten doughnuts, thanks for nothing," Dingdong replied. "Good job we brought our own." She opened her rucksack to reveal a picnic every bit as good as Baxter's.

Baxter and me climbed the tree, a bit more slowly now it was dark.

Baxter kept on grumbling, "I don't understand how they knew. How did they find us?"

"They didn't have to be Einstein to work that out," I told him.

I took the binoculars and scanned the area. The farm was in darkness, nothing to see there. My mum's bedroom light was on; she was probably reading in bed. There was nothing happening at Old Crumble's house. But then his lights went on and he opened his back door to let Brutus out for a last pee in the garden. His lights went out; Mum's light went out; Birdy's lights were already out.

We settled back and waited. Just when we were

starting to get bored again, Birdy's kitchen lights suddenly flicked on. I could see her, as plain as day through her kitchen window.

"What do you think she's up to," I said, "at this time of night?"

"Pass me the bins," Baxter said. He watched for a while in silence. "Definitely suspicious. She's up to no good. See that?" He passed the binoculars back to me.

"What?" I said. "Just looks like she's baking." Not exactly suspicious!

"In the middle of the night? And what about

those, there, on the worktop?" he said. I moved the binoculars along until I could see what looked like a whole stack of trays of eggs!

"There must be dozens of 'em!" Baxter said, excitedly. "There's your evidence."

So, it was Birdy all along, playing innocent, pretending to be a poor old pensioner. Then sneaking out in the night and nicking dozens of eggs. After days of watching a pair of dumb animals sleep and scratch themselves, here was some real criminal behaviour at last.

"I think we may have found our culprit," Baxter said, sounding like Sherlock Holmes wrapping up the case.

But I wanted to be absolutely sure.

"Perhaps we should get a closer look," I suggested.

"Ready when you are, Watson," Baxter agreed.

As soon as we climbed down the tree a full-scale argument broke out. Even though we didn't tell them what we'd seen, or where we were going, the other two were determined to come with us.

"But we're only going to have a look round," Baxter said. "Make sure it's safe for you two."

"Don't bother. I can look after myself," Dingdong told him.

"Me too," Sam said, bravely.

"Look," I said, "we need you to stay here and guard the camp. What if someone comes and nicks our stuff? And if anything happens to us we'll need back up. Have you got your phone?"

"'Course I've got my phone," Dingdong snapped.

"You know it makes good business sense," I told them. "It's called maximising our resources."

"Yes, yes, bor-ing. We get it," Dingdong said. "Just don't be long or we're coming to look for you."

"Fine," I said, "but keep quiet and try to stay out of trouble."

"Tttch. You're as bad as my mum," Dingdong complained.

"He's worse than ours," Sam added.

But I still wasn't happy leaving them. They hadn't even got Glenda the Defender to protect them. As we headed off, I said, "D'you think they'll really be OK?"

"Don't be such a girl," Baxter said, dismissively. "What can happen? Sam's fast and Dingdong's got a good pair of lungs."

But it was another of those times when I should have listened to my instincts.

I looked back, and saw them sitting there in the nearly dark, and something told me I'd be sorry about this.

And man, was I.

CHAPTER EIGHT

We hadn't brought our torches but there was enough moonlight to let us see the path. But when we reached Birdy's house, even on tiptoe, we couldn't see anything because of the blooming back hedge.

"You get down," Baxter whispered, "I'll stand on your back."

"You get lost," I said. I was way lighter than him.

Baxter grabbed me round my knees and lifted me off the ground. I snatched a glimpse of Birdy in her kitchen before I came crashing back to earth.

"You're heavier than you look," he said, panting.

"Maybe you're weaker," I said.

After we stopped bickering, I said, "This is a waste of time. We're hardly going to catch her in the act while she's baking."

"Maybe she'll go out stealing later," Baxter said.

I told him she wasn't exactly dressed for it. She was in a dressing gown, with curlers in her hair. "Unless," I said, "she's planning on scaring the chickens to death."

That made us both laugh, really quietly, but not quiet enough. Brutus suddenly set off barking inside the house. We dropped to the ground and held our breath.

"Perhaps we should go?" I whispered.

"Are you mad?" he whispered back. "There's a reason she's up at this time of night. We're going to find out what it is."

As soon as it was quiet again Baxter pointed to the apple tree that grows in the corner of Birdy's garden. It's so big it overhangs Old Crumble's too.

"You go first," he hissed, pushing me headlong through the hedge before following me.

Baxter gave me a leg up, then I reached down and gave him a pull. We both climbed higher until we reached a branch that gave us the best view into Birdy's kitchen.

Now we could see her quite clearly, with a pile

of white boxes lined up in front of her. What we couldn't see was what she was putting into them.

Baxter edged up closer. "Move over!" he whispered.

I slid further out along the branch than I was entirely happy with. It was pretty bouncy. I tried to steady myself. But just then I heard voices coming from the path behind us and I almost fell out of the tree.

"Where d'you think they are?" I heard Dingdong whisper. Not that Dingdong knows how to whisper!

"Search me," said Sam.

"I'll bet they're here somewhere," she said, flashing her torch around. Baxter and me flattened ourselves along the branch. We tried to stay like that, without moving, barely breathing. In the end it was Brutus that saved us. Dingdong had made such a fuss the dog started up again. It was enough to scare Dingdong and Sam off, back to the den if they had any sense.

Baxter and me returned to watching Birdy. She was carrying a yummy-looking cake onto the worktop.

"You see, she's only baking," I whispered to Baxter.

"The point still is," he replied, "where did she get all them eggs? Because she's only a poor pensioner," he added in Birdy's voice.

I sighed, he was probably right.

Suddenly a terrible piercing noise shattered the quiet. It was a mobile phone ringing. It took a few moments for me to realise it was my mobile phone and it was in my jeans pocket. It isn't easy getting into your jeans pocket when you're sitting precariously up a tree. I finally got it out.

"Who is it?" I hissed into the phone.

"It's me, of course, who do you think it is?"

"What do you want, Dingdong?" I said, irritably.

"Where are you?" she demanded.

Before I could answer, Birdy's back door opened. A face looked out, fearfully. "Who's there?" she called.

I quickly turned off the phone and again flattened myself to the branch. Baxter's breathing sounded deafening in my ear. I was sure she must be able to hear us.

"Whoever you are, I'm ringing the police," she called out.

Birdy went back inside and turned the key in the lock.

"Now what do we do?" I asked.

"Don't panic," was Baxter's helpful advice.

Panic! I was beyond panic. But I forced myself to wait…and wait…After a while I started to relax and to think we might have got away with it.

But then Birdy's back door opened and we almost fell out of the tree again. Birdy came out looking a lot braver, now that she wasn't alone. She wasn't alone because she had Dingdong and Sam with her! The doughnuts clearly hadn't gone back to the den!

"You're supposed to be Neighbourhood Watch," we heard Birdy tell them. "See what you can find."

"I can't see anyone," Dingdong said. "Perhaps you imagined it."

"I didn't imagine it. I heard someone," Birdy

insisted. "Shine that torch around."

Dingdong did as she was told, flashing her torch all round the garden. It didn't take her long to spot Baxter and me, hiding up the tree. She looked straight at us, and grinned.

But, luckily, Dingdong's no snitch.

"I'll bet I know what it was," we heard her tell Birdy. "A couple of those birds you're always feeding. A big fat pair probably roosting in your tree." She flapped her elbows and quietly clucked.

Birdy wasn't taken in. "Birds?! Talking on telephones? I don't think so. Give me that torch. I'll see for myself."

She tried to take the torch, but Dingdong clung onto it.

"Quick," she said, giving us a chance to escape. Baxter and me took it. We scrambled back towards the trunk and onto a branch where we might be more hidden.

But we were suddenly in the spotlight. Birdy had the torch now and it was trained straight onto us. She stared up into our faces.

"They're not birds!" we heard her exclaim.

I was in front of Baxter and almost blinded by the light. I tried to cover my eyes and that's when I lost my balance. As I started to fall I reached out and grabbed the closest thing to hand – Baxter.

Locked together, we fell out of the tree and over the fence, onto Old Crumble's side. We sailed straight through the top of his pride and joy: his shiny, new, state-of-the-art greenhouse. CRASH!!!

CHAPTER NINE

f I say so myself, it was a stroke of genius taking Baxter with me when I fell. It gave me something soft to land on.

Can you believe that both of us fell out of a tree and through a greenhouse and hardly broke anything? Well, apart from an arm – and a leg, in Baxter's case. But that's nothing, is it? We thought we'd got off pretty lightly – for all of two minutes. Then the nightmare really started.

Old Crumble's back door opened, and the garden was flooded with light. A yelping, snarling, panting, slavering monster hurled itself against the greenhouse door. Every pane of glass that wasn't already broken rattled and so did our teeth.

Even as Old Crumble turned the handle, I kept on praying, please, please, don't open the door. I lay on a bed of broken tomato plants thinking, what a waste! To die so young, with all that business potential still not realised.

Baxter and I tried to get up, but we were so scared neither of us could move.

"It was good knowing you, Banksy," Baxter whimpered.

"You, too, Dude," I whimpered back.

We closed our eyes and waited to be savaged.

But to our amazement – and relief – there was no pain. No savaging, anyway. Just toxic fumes! Blasts of hot, manky breath as a disgusting flabby tongue licked us all over. It was brutal!

Just when I thought I'd die from the smell

itself, Brutus planted his paws on my chest and gave my face a final good lathering! My stomach heaved.

As Baxter said later, the army could bottle Brutus's breath and use it as a weapon of mass destruction.

But even in my concussed state I realised what a fast one Old Crumble had pulled on us all this time. He'd let us think Brutus is potentially the most dangerous dog alive. When the truth is he's nothing but a big stinky wuss!

I got a small revenge, though. I rolled over and was disgustingly sick all over Old Crumble's prize geraniums.

After that things got a bit confused. I don't remember getting out, but the next thing I was sitting on the grass with my head between my knees. Everyone was there: Birdy stood over me in her dressing gown, asking me if I was OK. Dingdong was still holding the guilty torch and Sam was beside her, grinning. He does that when he's nervous. Baxter was next to me with bits of tomato plants still stuck to him.

And Old Crumble was asking me, "What on God's green earth were you doing up the tree in the first place?"

"Leave the boy alone," Birdy said. "He's in shock!"

84

"I'm in shock, too," Baxter insisted, but no one seemed bothered about him.

"Oh, my goodness, is that blood?" Birdy suddenly shrieked.

Everyone looked down at me, and then at Baxter. We were both covered in red sticky goo. I was about to faint, I think, until Baxter put his hand to his mouth and licked it. "Tomato," he said. "Yum, very tasty, Mr Crump."

Old Crumble nearly burst a blood vessel at that point. "Will one of you explain to me what you were doing up a tree in the middle of the night."

"We were just trying to find out what Birdy was up to with all those eggs," Baxter started to explain.

"Eggs? What eggs?" Old Crumble asked, bewildered.

"All those stacks of eggs she's got," Baxter said.

"What's it got to do with you?" Birdy asked.

85

"Can't a poor pensioner sell a few cakes to make a bob or two?"

Old Crumble was still struggling to see how Birdy and eggs and cakes had led to Baxter and me falling through his greenhouse in the middle of the night. I had to agree; it wasn't an obvious chain of events.

Then Dingdong, who was feeling partly to blame, told Birdy, "They probably thought you were my dad's egg thief. They were only trying to solve the crime…"

I let her rabbit on a bit, but in the end I told them, "It all started because Mr Crump wanted evidence about you and your bread, and you wanted proof he was putting poo over your fence."

That shut them both up. They looked amazed – and embarrassed. "It was later we got on to the eggs," I said.

"That still doesn't explain what you were doing

in my garden," Old Crumble blustered a bit more.

But Birdy told him to be quiet. "They're just kids," she said. "We're the adults, we're the ones who ought to have known better! Falling out about bread – and dog poo!"

Old Crumble looked down, he didn't try to deny it.

It was at this point Baxter tried to get up. When his leg wouldn't hold him, he capsized onto me. It was when I tried to push him up I realised my

arm didn't usually bend that way. Then everyone looked a lot more guilty.

"See what's happened to these poor boys, all because of our stupidity," Birdy said. "They both need to get to hospital."

"I'll get dressed and take them," Old Crumble volunteered.

Birdy said, "Annabelle, go next door and wake Robin's mum."

"Oh, no, don't do that, please," I begged. But even I knew I was wasting my breath. I suspected I wasn't going to hear the end of this for a very long time.

Baxter's mum took him to the hospital in their van, so he had more room to stretch his leg out. Mum bundled me into Old Crumble's car without a word. But I knew this was the calm before the tornado heading my way anytime soon.

Baxter and me sat together in the hospital waiting room. But the grown-ups kept giving us really cold looks, so we hardly dared to speak above a whisper.

And after everything that had happened, do you know what was the main thing on Baxter's mind? Food!

"I hope they still let us have our camping breakfast when we get home," he whispered.

"In your dreams," I whispered back.

"Those big fat sausages going to waste!" he whined. "Tragic!"

In the car going home Mum was still giving me the big chill. But now I had a brilliant shiny white plaster cast to cheer me up. It looked like newly fallen snow, just ready and waiting…

I knew something good had to come out of this latest disaster. Some new business possibility. Oh, yes, I thought, watch this space.

CHAPTER TEN

You know what it's like when there's obviously an idea there, some real potential, but you can't see it? At times like that I always ask myself: W-W-L-S-D? What Would Lord Sugar Do?

It's like I try to channel him. And just like that the idea came to me!

We weren't stupid. Over the next week we all knew to lay low where our mums, and the neighbours, were concerned. Even though Baxter was on crutches we spent everyday in the park. But this gave us a chance to develop my new mini business idea.

I always like to think I have a nose for a deal.
Well, this time I had an arm for it, as well. And
Baxter had a leg! We called the business: Left Arm
and Leg Ads.

To begin with people were a bit slow to fork
out their pocket money. But those two spotless
white surfaces were just too tempting and in the
end people were queuing up.

First, a couple of the footballers bought a 5cms
square to advertise their football boots for sale.
Brenda Gull posted a message about her missing
moggy. She did a pretty good drawing of it too. Jake

Johnson used Baxter's leg to look for a new goalie. Sam even advertised his baby guinea pigs for sale. After that we were almost fighting people off.

Even when Brenda Gull's cat turned up – well, not exactly turned up because a No 9 bus had run it over – we didn't have to waste the space. We painted over it with Tippex and resold it to a boy who needed the last card to finish his football collection.

In the end we made a grand total of ten pounds fifty.

Not a fortune, I know, but we'd barely had to lift a finger! Or, as Baxter pointed out, even a toe!

Obviously, ten pounds fifty didn't begin to pay for all the broken panes in Old Crumble's greenhouse. That's probably going to take us for ever to pay for. But we did get a bit of extra dosh from Dingdong. Dingdong was still feeling guilty that it had been partly her fault that we'd fallen out of the tree. If they'd been been back at the den, instead of wandering round the car park when Birdy came looking for help, they wouldn't have got dragged into it.

Baxter and me let Dingdong go on feeling guilty. We reckoned she owed us the extra pocket money she finally got for clearing up the mystery of her dad's stolen eggs.

It turns out that after Baxter and me had been taken off to the hospital, Dingdong and Sam had their own adventure.

When they went back to the den to collect all the gear, they suddenly heard noises, something like the ones we'd heard. As if someone was dragging something along the ground. In our case it had been those two doughnuts, with their rucksacks. This time it really was wild animals: a pair of foxes.

"Of course it was a fox," Baxter interrupted the story. "Bound to be. I could have told you that!" I thought it was a pity he hadn't. It might have saved us a broken arm and leg!

Apparently, Sam and Dingdong had ducked inside the den, just like we had. Luckily this time nobody stuck their heads inside.

"But there are some great big holes in that den," Dingdong said, critically, "so we could see the

foxes as clear as anything. Their mouths were full of dead chickens!"

Dingdong said Sam had been in a kind of trance, seeing the foxes so close. But she'd been on the ball.

"The minute they moved off we went straight to the chicken run. We followed the trail of feathers," she said, proudly. "That's how we found where they'd got in. It was the tiniest gap in the fence. My dad had searched and hadn't been able to find it. But we did."

The best thing was he'd kept his promise and paid up. Now Dingdong waved the tenner under our noses. "You can put it towards Old Crumble's greenhouse fund," she said.

"Thanks," I said, about to take it off her.

But Baxter said, "Hang on. You do realise we're going to be stony broke all summer?"

"Tell me something I don't know," I replied.

"We don't have to put that tenner in the greenhouse fund," he said, craftily. "No one needs to know."

We all looked at each other. "So what would we do with it instead?" Dingdong asked, suspiciously.

Before I had the chance to suggest investing it in our next business project, Baxter said, "We could have a cook-out, at the den." He was still banging on about that cooked breakfast he'd missed having.

It was a no-brainer to think we might be allowed to stay out overnight again. But it was just possible we could have a picnic, I suggested.

"What kind of picnic?" Dingdong asked, suspiciously.

"Leave that to me," said Baxter. "I'll take care of everything."

Dingdong and me shared a look, but in the end we coughed up the lolly and left him to it. After all, with a broken arm and leg between us, we weren't likely to have much more fun this summer holiday.

The next afternoon we sat down by the stream while Baxter cooked hotdogs and onions on a camping stove. Dingdong tucked them into baps and Sam covered them in tomato ketchup. And what did I do? I ate them, of course. Well, I did have a broken arm!

They were probably the best hot dogs I'd ever had!

"You know what," I said. "These hotdogs are good enough to…"

"Eat?" said Baxter.

"I was going to say, sell." Baxter and me started to grin. "How much d'you reckon we could charge?" I was doing some quick sums in my head.

Dingdong narrowed her eyes. "Look, I'm not saying these aren't brilliant hotdogs, but…"

"But what?"

Dingdong sighed. "You know what you're like. You'll probably end up setting the whole place on fire, including us. And when it happens just remember: I was the one who said it would. OK?"

And you know what…

But I'll save that story, The Bogie of Doom – and how it all went up in flames – for another time.

For now, Adiós Amigos.

The Bogie of
Doom

Rose Impey

CHAPTER ONE

I bet I know what you've come back for: *the full fireworks.*

The barely-believable-but-true story of the burning of the *Bogie of Doom*. That was epic.

If it weren't for that disaster we could have been seriously rich. I mean minting it, not to mention beating the girls at their own game. With Baxter cooking, I guess I should have seen it coming. But I didn't and my only excuse was the heat.

It was the very end of August, the last week of the holidays. Thank goodness we had both finally got our plasters off. We'd been itching and sweating inside them all summer.

It was so hot it felt like your brain was melting. Even the surface of the car park was sticking to our trainers. Baxter and me were so bored we were picking bits off and flicking them at each other. My mum had to cut whole chunks out of my hair.

"This is truly *dis-gusting*, Robin," she complained.

If she thinks this is disgusting, I thought, she

should see Baxter's usual *pick it-lick it-flick it* trick!
I told you he has seriously *bad* habits!

Anyway, we weren't bored for much longer.
The next morning workmen came to dig up the
lane, to lay some new drains. The minute we heard
the lorries arrive we raced over to get a front row
seat. Glenda the Defender was living up to her
name, barking fit to burst. As usual, no one took
any notice of her.

Dingdong wasn't around. She was having a
sleepover with Horseface. You might remember
the dreaded Nigella Horseforth. Like Baxter says,
"If it looks like a horse and it sounds like a horse,
it's sure to be a horse." So that's what we call her.

This was the first time Dingdong had been
invited back to Nigella's house since the famous
wedding haircut. Remember that story? Sweet
revenge!

It was a good thing. If Dingdong *had* been

around, she'd only have been bored and bugging us every five minutes wanting to know: *what now?* Diggers are definitely *a boy thing*.

So for the next hour we watched a huge great excavator ripping chunks out of the lane. We sat back with our drinks and packets of crisps like we were at the cinema. There was a small gang of men following the digger with shovels. Sweat was pouring off them even though it was still early in the morning.

"Makes me hot just watching 'em," said Baxter, eating his last mouthful of crisps. He'd scoffed the packet in record time: two and a half mouthfuls.

"Hurry up, you two," he told Sam and me. Every packet had a ticket inside. He'd already checked his packet without luck. "Come on! We could win £1000!" he said, excitedly.

I thought, in your dreams.

"Have you any idea what the odds are against

winning?" I asked Baxter. I didn't know either to be honest, but I made a number up. "Probably ten million to one. It's like the lottery, one big con."

"Yeah, well, not if you're the lucky one. And it's the only way we're ever going to hit the jackpot," he grumbled.

Baxter and me had had this argument a hundred times but that didn't stop us having it again.

"In business you create your own luck," I reminded him, "with hard work and red-hot ideas. And since there's only a week of the holidays left, we need to come up with one, *pronto*."

Baxter yawned and burped. Very helpful, I thought.

Just then the digger driver took a break and one of the workmen called us over. He offered us a pound if we'd go to the local shop to get them some cold bottles of pop.

We didn't mind; we'd nothing better to do. Baxter and me collected our BMXs and raced up there. We brought back five bottles. It was hot work for me, because I was the one carrying all the extra weight. Baxter – The Great Explorer – doesn't even have a saddlebag.

He wanted to spend the pound in the shop, but I quickly reminded him our readies were at an all time low.

"We need to build up some capital for our next

business venture," I told him.

"Whatever that might be," Baxter said, sarcastically.

Little did we realise the idea would be waiting for us, when we got back.

While we'd been gone the place had filled up with kids. Most were from school: Jake Johnson and half the football team, plus some other hangers-on. Matt Biggs and his mates stood leaning on their bikes and staring like they'd never seen men at work before.

"What are you lot doing here?" they asked, as if it wasn't bloomin' obvious. It is our lane after all.

"This and that," Baxter mumbled, vaguely. "And, before you ask, no, you can't."

That crowd's always trying to get into The Get Rich Quick Club. As if. Let's face it: if we needed the heavy mob, we've already got Baxter.

All the kids watched the workmen drink the

cold pop. Their tongues were literally hanging out, like it was the last liquid this side of the desert.

And that's when the idea came to me...

"Quick, let's get back to the shed," I hissed, dragging Baxter and Sam to one side. I winked, to let them know I'd got something good cooking.

They weren't exactly quick to catch on.

"What for?" they grumbled, playing *Dumb and Even Dumber*. Not hard parts for the Baxters.

"A *board* meeting," I said, meaningfully.

"What board?" Sam asked as we headed back.

"The board of the brand-spanking-new *Superior Snack Bar Company*," I announced grandly.

"The what?" Sam asked, as clueless as ever, but Baxter was beginning to catch on.

"Snack Bar! Nice one, Banksy," he agreed and we high-fived.

"Come on," I told Sam, "you'll see," and I opened the shed door and led them inside.

I was still working it all out in my head as I talked. But I knew this was going to be another gold-plated winner. Our new pop-up business scheme was already on its way to going live. As easy as that.

I know, I know! Sometimes I can't believe how brilliant I am, either.

CHAPTER TWO

I always say that the most important thing in business is: *ideas, ideas, ideas*. But it's just as important to make things happen. You'll never get the readies if you're all talk and no action.

Luckily, *The Get Rich Quick* Club talks the talk *and* walks the walk. And today, we were *sprinting*! For the next hour we raced round begging and borrowing…OK, maybe a tiny bit of stealing, too. Only a few cup hooks to hang the snacks on, not exactly a hanging offence.

Then we carried everything we'd collected

up the lane: Baxter's wallpapering table, Mum's kitchen stool, every cup, mug and beaker we could lay our hands on, blah, blah, blah...

By the time the other kids came back from lunch we were open for business. *Da daa!* Pretty impressive, huh!

I'd cycled up to the shop. Thanks to a shortage of funds all we could afford were two giant bottles of fizz. But, as I always say: *Start small, think big* and see where it leads.

After all, even McDonalds had to start somewhere!

"How much're we charging?" Baxter whispered, as the customers began to queue up.

I shrugged. "20p a cup?" It seemed fair and we'd still make a big fat profit on each bottle.

But then I hadn't exactly planned for the fact that the cups were all different sizes. A fight almost broke out between Matt Biggs, who had a paper cup, and Jake Johnson, who had somehow got hold of Baxter's toothbrush mug.

"This piddling little thing only holds half as much as his big fat mug," Matt complained. "How's that fair?"

Of course, it wasn't fair. But a free refill managed to calm Biggsy down. Then there was the problem of Baxter's aim.

"Whoa! Whoa! Whoa!" I yelled as I watched our profits pouring off the table. "It's meant to go *in* the cups!"

"These big bottles weigh a ton," Baxter grumbled.

But finally his aim improved and after that we were on a roll. I was soon riding up to the shop for fresh supplies. Crisps and snacks as well this time. Of course, that meant leaving Baxter in charge. Always a risky business.

Here's another useful business tip: *It never pays to be greedy.* Value for money has always been one of my mottos. Pity it's not one of Baxter's.

While I was away, he had the bright idea of watering down the Coke. Have you ever tasted watered Coke? It's pants! He was lucky he didn't get it poured over his head.

"You're always telling me to maximize profits," he growled.

"Not if it causes a riot," I growled back.

But free replacements calmed things down

again. The one thing about Baxter is he soon gets over himself. The next time I looked he was pouring a bit of this and a bit of that into a paper cup.

"What're you up to now? I hope you're not drinking our profits," I warned him.

Baxter gave me one of his mysterious looks. The next time I went for supplies, he gave me a long list of different drinks to bring back.

"What do we want all these for?"

"Just do the shopping, Banksy. Leave the creative stuff to me."

I went off to the shop wondering what he'd got planned this time. When I got back a new sign had appeared: *Baxter's Monster Mixes.*

He grinned and handed me a paper cup. After I drank out of it I couldn't speak for a whole minute. But I had to admit, it was *lethal.* "What d'you call that?" I spluttered.

"*The Choker,*" Baxter said proudly.

There were others: *The Hammer, ShockerRocker, Blast Off* and finally… *Whodunnit?* I didn't even try that one! I just prayed there'd be no bodies to identify afterwards.

Sam had been sent home to collect more stuff: spoons, his mum's whisk, and a flask that Baxter was now using as a cocktail shaker.

"You could get a job in a cocktail bar when you're older," one of the workmen told Baxter. The compliment went straight to his head. He started doing all this silly business, shaking the flask like a pair of maracas. He plucked a few flowers out

of the hedge and stuck them in the drinks like cocktail umbrellas.

By the end of the day it was official: *Baxter's Monster Mixes* were a sell-out success. Kids had been cycling home to get more money. We'd made a profit of twelve pounds, in just a couple of hours. It was mental!

We took the stall down and carried everything back to the shed. We sat in the sun finishing off the opened bottles and celebrating our first day in the snack bar business.

Baxter let out an epic burp. "Good work," he told himself. Then an even bigger one. "Beat that if you can," he grinned.

I tried, but Baxter's the undisputed King of Wind. Either end, no one competes with The Dude.

Baxter and me had an argument then over whether to eat the last three packets of crisps. I pointed out it was our profits we'd be eating. "We'll only have to buy more stock tomorrow," I said.

"Not if the winning ticket's in there," he said, excitedly.

"We stand more chance of finding a foreign body in those packets than the winning ticket," I told Baxter.

"What kind of foreign body?" he asked, intrigued.

"I dunno, some bug or beetle, or somebody's toenail," I said.

"I read about a woman who found a mouse in a tin of baked beans. They gave her a big payout so she wouldn't sue."

"What happened to the mouse, Banksy?" Sam asked.

"It was dead, Sam," I said. "It was in a tin of baked beans!"

He looked like he might be about to cry.

"Calm down," Baxter told him. "It's just one of Banksy's stories," as if I'd made it up specially to scare Sam. He gave me a warning look.

I agreed. "It was probably just a story, Sam."

And Sam immediately cheered up.

So then we ate the crisps and everyone cheered up.

The reality was we'd got a nice little money-earner started already. We hadn't made a lot yet, but sometimes, in business, *slow and steady's the winning formula*. You've heard of the Hare and the Tortoise, right?

Hmmm, well, unfortunately, Baxter hadn't.

CHAPTER THREE

The next day we had our snack bar up and running before nine o'clock. We were even better organised as we squeezed together under Baxter's mum's sunshade. Word seemed to have got round because even more kids arrived. Baxter said it was the digger they'd come for, but *I* knew the snack bar was the main attraction.

Baxter started bragging about the deal he'd made with a friend of Wayne's. His name was Chuck and he had a market stall. "He's letting us have a couple of boxes of crisps – *dead cheap.*"

Baxter added, casually, "You know, as a favour."

I could smell something rotten straight away, and it wasn't pickled onion. But Baxter told me to stop being such a girl. "After all," he said, "we're paying next to nothing for them." When the crisps arrived it was obvious why. They were two months past their sell-by date.

"So? So!" Baxter gave me a pitying look. "Who looks at sell-by dates?" he started to cluck. "Apart from chickens!"

I shrugged and just kept my fingers crossed that no one died of food poisoning.

We were still making most of our money on the drinks. But, to be fair to Baxter, as the morning went on, we did a brisk trade in crisps too. And he was right, none of the kids even looked at the sell-by date.

Of course, Baxter wasn't only thinking about our profit. Every time anyone bought a packet

Baxter snatched it out of his hand, almost before he'd finished the last mouthful.

"I'll take that, thank you very much," he said menacingly, like he was the Litter Police.

By the end of the morning he'd collected a pocketful of coupons. "Maybe this'll increase our odds," he said, waving them under my nose.

"Yeah, now we're really in with a chance," I said, sarcastically. "It's probably gone down to…nine million to one."

Baxter looked crushed for a moment, but he was soon planning his revenge.

"Why don't you take a break, Banksy?" he said later on. "Here, have a crisp." He held out a packet he'd just opened.

"No, thanks," I said.

"Just one," he said, waving the packet under my nose. "That nice big one on top. It's got your name on, *Robin*."

That made me suspicious. Baxter *never* calls me by my real name. Luckily, I wasn't hungry.

Two minutes later he let out this dramatic groan, and clutched his stomach. "Oh, no! I don't believe it. Yuk!" Considering he's such a poser, Baxter's a rubbish actor.

"What? What is it, Baxter?" Sam asked, anxiously.

"THAT SURE DOESN'T LOOK LIKE A CRISP TO ME," Baxter said, like he was talking in capital letters.

I finally gave in and peered into the packet. On top was this big scabby-looking crisp, a bit *redder*

than the others. I knew straight away what it was.

A week ago, the very day Baxter had his plaster off, he fell out of a tree. He'd been saving that scab on his knee ever since. It was probably some kind of record for him.

"Oh, no!" he said, still acting up. "That's *disgusting.*"

"*You're* disgusting," I said looking down at his knee and the patch of shiny new pink skin.

Baxter burst out laughing. "Had you going there for a minute, though, didn't I?" he said proudly.

I gave a weary sigh and let him enjoy his big scabby joke.

So, even later, in the afternoon, when Sam started, I thought: here we go again. "Change the record," I told him.

"No, honest, Banksy," Sam insisted. "I just bit on it. It must have been in the packet, I swear it."

It was a tooth and it looked human. Even I had to admit it was far too big to have come out of Sam's mouth. Imagining how the tooth might have got in there made me feel a bit sick to be honest. I thought I'll never eat another crisp again.

But you know Baxter, he even finished the packet the tooth had been in. "When you've survived in the wild," he shrugged, "you can't afford to be squeamish."

I was sure the two of them had set me up, although Sam insisted he hadn't. He said he might put the tooth in his gruesome collection. But in the end I gave him 50p for it.

I didn't tell Sam or Baxter what I wanted it for. I don't tell Baxter everything, you know.

But for now we had a business to run and the next two hours went pretty well. We'd made £12 the first day, £25 already today. *If* the weather stayed this hot, and *if* the workmen stuck around, we could be looking at serious smackers.

But you know what they say about counting your chickens?

We suddenly noticed the sound of the diggers had stopped. When we looked over we saw a couple of official-looking men staring down a big hole. All the workmen were leaning on their shovels watching them.

"That doesn't look good," said Baxter.

It was gone four o'clock and, with nothing much going on, the other kids drifted off home. Soon the men packed up too. Then the whole area was roped off. Apparently they'd dug into some old mine workings.

"There's a real danger of subsidence," one of the men told us, "so you kids are going to have to keep well away from here from now on."

"You'll be back tomorrow, though?" Baxter asked, hopefully, but we all knew the answer.

As fast as that, the bottom fell out of our solid gold-plated business. We were gutted. When we got back to the shed, we thought this was as bad as it could get. But we were wrong.

Just then Dingdong came home – and guess who she'd brought with her. Our least favourite person in the whole wide world: Nigella *Horseface* Horseforth. The Medusa in disguise.

Baxter and me did the crossed fingers sign – to ward off vampires. It may work on vampires, but we clearly needed something much stronger to repel the Medusa in disguise.

CHAPTER FOUR

"Y ou should call this *The Get Lost Quick Club*," Horseface said. "Or even better *The Biggest Losers' Club*." She laughed like a horse at her own jokes.

Everyone ignored her, including Dingdong.

"What've you lot been up to?" Dingdong asked us.

So we gave her a quick rundown of everything she'd missed. We told her about the workmen, the kids from school and the small fortune we'd started to make on our snack bar.

"I bet they didn't make as much money as us," Horseface said to Dingdong.

"We've been helping Nigella's mum," Dingdong explained, "baking and selling stuff."

"For charity," Horseface added, smugly.

"I thought about doing a bit of baking," Baxter announced, grandly. It was the first I'd heard of it. "You know, to sell on our snack bar, if we hadn't gone out of business," he added.

Dingdong and Horseface started giggling. I almost joined in. The idea of Baxter baking *was* pretty hilarious. Good job I didn't.

"I don't know what you two find so amusing," he snapped.

"In case you hadn't noticed, all the top chefs are *men*." He listed some of the ones on TV. "Jamie Oliver, Gordon Ramsay, Hugh Fearnley...Doodah-What's his Name..."

"What about Delia, the queen of them all?"

Dingdong asked.

"And Nigella?" Horseface added. "I don't mean me, of course," she giggled. "I mean the *lovely* Nigella Lawson."

Baxter and me pretended to vomit.

"There may be *more* men," Dingdong conceded, "but that's cos men get on everything, cos they're bigger show-offs. And being a show-off doesn't always mean you're good at something, does it, *Baxter*?" she added, pointedly.

I didn't bother joining in. It was their usual boring argument: *who's better, girls or boys?* It quickly turned personal.

"I could cook *you* for Sunday dinner," Baxter told Dingdong.

"I could cook *you* under the table," Dingdong replied.

"*You* couldn't boil an egg."

"*You* couldn't peel a potato."

In the end, they agreed, there was only one way to decide: *The Battle of the Bakers*. This'll be epic, I thought.

"Girls versus boys, then," Dingdong said.

"Bring it on," said Baxter.

"But there's three of them," Nigella quickly pointed out. "That's hardly fair. Although I suppose that one only counts as a half…or a quarter," she added, grinning nastily at Sam.

"It's fine," Dingdong said, dismissing her. "Baxter needs all the help he can get. So, what's the prize going to be?"

I looked at Baxter. I didn't mind him having a pointless battle with Dingdong. I didn't even mind being dragged into it. But there was no way he was going to gamble our hard-earned snack bar money on it.

Baxter shrugged; he didn't seem to care as long as he won. But Dingdong had a crafty look in her eye. "Whoever loses," she announced, "will be Slaves for a Day."

"Oh, sweet," said Baxter, already imagining the terrible things he would heap on the girls' heads. But I was stuck in the nightmare possibility of being Slave for a Day to Nigella Horseforth. This couldn't be allowed to happen. We needed to square things up a bit – and fast.

"Hang on," I said, taking charge. "Let's make it like *The Apprentice*."

The Apprentice is my all-time favourite TV programme. Lord Sugar gives everyone these challenges to see who can make the most money for him. "We each make stuff and then sell it," I said. "Whoever makes the biggest profit wins. Simple."

"Suits me," said Dingdong.

"Ready when you are," said Baxter.

"But now the workmen are gone," Sam pointed out, "who are we going to sell to?"

He had a point. Now the road show was over, the kids had gone too. They'd all be back on the park. That's where we'd hold our *Big Hard Sell*, two o'clock tomorrow afternoon. It was all agreed.

"Let the best team win," I said, shaking hands with Dingdong.

"Oh, we will," laughed Baxter.

"In your dreams," Dingdong said, quietly, staring me in the eye. She had a look of total, all-out confidence on her face that made me nervous.

I think I've told you before, by far the most

irritating thing about Dingdong is how often she turns out to be right. Not this time, I prayed. Please, not this time.

"Come on, Nigella, we'd better get started," she said.

"Yes, see you in the park, *losers*," Nigella told us, nastily.

After they'd gone, we sat around for a while, no one saying anything. In the end I couldn't help myself. "Baxter...what if we lose?"

"We won't lose," he said, perfectly seriously.

"But how can you be so sure?"

"Do you know the big difference between girls and boys?" Baxter asked, with an evil grin. "When the chips are down, *boys play dirty*. So we'll start with a little industrial espionage. You're going to spy on the girls," he told me, "and report back at..." he looked at his watch, "1900 hours."

"Why me?" I asked.

"Oh, Bluey. Because no one'll suspect you. You're the nice guy, remember?"

And he was right, I am. As much as I wanted to win, as much as we *needed* to win, I hate cheating. I stood there dithering.

"For goodness sake, Banksy," Baxter groaned. "Just find out what they're making, will you? It's not exactly international spying."

I went home for supper first and ate three helpings of lasagne. I wasn't that hungry, but I was in no hurry to go out. In the end I couldn't put it off any longer.

I went over to the farm and sneaked round the side of the house. It was still steaming hot and all the windows and doors were open. Amazing smells were coming from the kitchen. When I looked in I thought, "Man, are we stuffed!"

It was like a little factory. There were rows

of cupcakes on the table. Dingdong and Nigella were icing them with different coloured icing, then sprinkling stuff on top. The cakes looked *professional*. You could just tell they'd taste like heaven on a plate. Even after three helpings of lasagne, I'd have wolfed half a dozen down given the chance.

I groaned and went straight back to give Baxter the bad news: short of a miracle, we should prepare to be walked all over – *by girls*.

CHAPTER FIVE

Baxter didn't seem at all worried, but I was. In business, another important thing to remember is: *Never underestimate the competition.*

OK, they might be girls, but they were going to take some beating. Why couldn't Baxter see that?

"Calm down, dear!" he told me. "Don't get your boxers up your bum." He hardly even looked up from leafing through one of his mum's cookery books. "You see, Banksy," *he* had the nerve to tell *me*, "in business, it's all about *profit margins*."

"I'm always telling *you* that!" I spluttered.

"So forget pretty cupcakes!" he carried on. "Bigger cakes, that's the answer. They'll be less work and, if we cut 'em salami-style, that means more slices. And that means more wonga for the work." He held out his arms as if he'd just single-handedly solved the eternal problems of the universe. "Genius or what!"

"But we *still* have to make the rotten cakes," I stressed.

"You worry too much," Baxter said, closing the book with a snap. "Leave the baking to me," he grinned. "It'll be a *piece of cake!*"

The next morning I was late going round to Baxter's. I hadn't slept very well.

"You look terrible," Mum told me.

"I had this nightmare," I said. "We were all in the park and Nigella and Dingdong made buckets of money selling donkey rides."

"Why's that a nightmare?" she asked.

"Guess who were the donkeys?" I said.

I passed Baxter's mum going off supermarket shopping, taking the baby with her. "Morning, Robin," she said, smiling. There was only one reason she could be looking that happy: she had no idea what Baxter was planning.

Sure enough, he met me at the door waving a shopping list. "We've got two hours, tops," he said, "before Mum gets back. We need these extra ingredients. Now, *go, go, go...*"

It isn't far to the local shop, but when I got there Dingdong and Horseface were inside. They were buying more decorations for their perfect cupcakes. I had to wait ages, pretending to look at sports magazines, until they left. So, even though it was another sweltering hot day, I broke all records racing home. When I reached Baxter's kitchen door and looked inside, I don't mind admitting I nearly ran away.

I know Baxter better than anyone; I know what he's capable of. But even *I* couldn't believe the *mon-u-mental* mess he'd made in such a short time.

He didn't hear me arrive because he'd got his mum's mixer going. He was mixing icing and, it was flying everywhere. He was wearing a fair amount of it. He looked like the Abominable Snowman – in camo gear!

On the plus side, there was a definite smell of baking. So some cake mixture must have actually got into the oven.

"Don't stand there slacking, Banksy," Baxter said, suddenly spotting me. "There's work to be done you know."

I put the shopping down in the one clear spot on the floor.

There were a couple of very thin, over-baked cakes already cooling on the table. Baxter took the icing he'd been making and spread a dollop on each cake.

"Mmm…mmm," he said, trying out half a handful.

"I'll have some, Baxter," Sam said. Sam was kneeling on a chair at the sink, bravely trying to keep up with the washing up. Judging by the colour of the water, he'd been using the same bowl over and over again.

I wondered when Baxter might notice the burning smell coming from the oven. Not soon enough. I rushed over and threw open the oven door. Smoke billowed out and set off the smoke alarms.

"Aww, Sa-a-am," Baxter yelled, putting his hands – still full of icing – to his head. "I told you to put the timer on!" He grabbed a newspaper and flapped it at the alarm sensor.

"Thought I had," Sam mumbled, through a mouthful of icing.

The alarm finally stopped. Baxter picked up his mum's oven gloves and lifted the burnt cinders out of the oven. He put them on the table with the others. They made the first ones look almost appetizing.

"No one'll notice," he said, "when they're covered with icing."

I rolled my eyes but didn't say anything. I left

the expert to get on with the baking and took a turn at the sink. I'd hardly made much impression when we heard a car arriving in the car park.

"Uh, oh, Mum's back early," Sam said.

I looked over at Baxter and saw a rare glimpse of panic on his face. He quickly covered it up with a careless shrug.

I put my head down and kept on washing up. When Baxter's mum walked into the kitchen I felt the temperature rise another ten degrees!

The fire alarm had been deafening, but it was nothing compared to Carol's screams when she saw the state of her kitchen. She only stopped screaming when the baby started crying.

"Out! Out! All of you!" she yelled, pointing a finger in the direction of the door.

"We were only doing a bit of baking," Baxter explained, trying to calm her down. "It's not like we'd set the house on fire."

"Not yet, you hadn't," she screamed. "Who knows what would have happened if I hadn't forgotten my credit cards. This is positively THE END of you and your baking career, Billy Baxter. I don't ever want you in my kitchen again. Understand? You are TOTALLY BANNED! FOR EVER."

We retired to the shed until things calmed down.

"So where will you eat your meals now?" I asked Baxter. I was being serious. They all have their meals in the kitchen, after all.

"Until this blows over, he'll probably get his outside in one of the dog bowls," Sam grinned. Baxter grinned too, but I wasn't grinning.

"In two hours we've got to be in the park, selling against the girls," I said. "And all we've got to sell are four burnt...*pancakes*!"

Baxter suddenly turned to me and smiled. "Oh, nice one, Banksy," he said.

"*Nice one?*" I repeated, thinking he must be finally losing it.

"You've just given me the best idea," Baxter told me, excitedly. "I want you and Sam to go and fetch the *Bogie of Doom*. We're going to need it to carry all the gear."

"Gear! What gear?" I asked, getting more and more frantic.

I could almost feel Nigella Horseforth already on my back.

"You'll see," Baxter said. "You leave it to me. We've got this competition…*in the pan!*"

CHAPTER 6

We found the *Bogie of Doom* at the back of the Baxters' garage. Baxter's dad had made it for us out of a set of old pram wheels and a couple of crates. We spent the whole of last summer riding it down Moss Bank. It was totally wild!

We made loads of dough charging 20p a go. That was until two kids from school fell off and broke things. Just an arm and a tooth, you know, nothing major! But after that it was BANNED.

I helped Sam wheel it round to the shed now. Apart from squeaking a bit, it seemed to be in working order.

I know Lord Sugar started off selling out of the back of his car, but I still couldn't see how the *Bogie of Doom* was going to save us. With less than an hour before *The Big Hard Sell* I was getting pretty jumpy.

Baxter finally appeared hidden behind a mound of stuff: a camping stove, spoons, whisks, bowls and a big heavy frying pan. Under his arm he had a piece of wood the size of a small table top.

"What's all this?" I asked.

"The gear," he said, loading it into the back of the bogie. "Everything we need…well, almost

everything…to make mouthwatering *c-rrrepes*," he said with a really bad French accent. "They're pancakes, you know."

"Yes, I do know that! I'm not stupid. But you said *almost* everything we need. What else?" I asked, suspiciously.

"Yeah, well, we still need a couple of ingredients."

I could see another high-speed bike ride coming up. "What do we need and where's the money?" I asked.

"Hmmm, well, there's the catch," said Baxter, looking around like he was searching for inspiration.

"Catch? What catch?" I asked, suspiciously.

In the end Sam grassed him up. "There's no money left," he said. "He gave it all to Old Birdy."

"Old Birdy?" I said, totally confused.

Baxter shrugged. "To rent me a frying pan and

the rest of the gear."

"You used *all* our money," I spluttered, "to rent a *frying pan*!"

"You can't make pancakes without one," Baxter argued. "And, look, it's top of the range: cast iron base, non-stick lining…" He waved the pan around, like he was advertising it on TV.

I was seriously tempted to test out the cast-iron base – on Baxter's head!

In fact, I was so mad, I pointed my finger, just like Lord Sugar. "You're fired," I told him. "F-I-R-E-D. *Fired!*" I'd been wanting to say that for such a long time.

"OK," Baxter shrugged. He sat down and took out his knife and a piece of wood. "But you might want to think about waiting to fire me until *after The Big Hard Sell*. Unless, of course, you secretly want to be Horseface's slave for the day." Then he returned to his favourite occupation: *whittling*.

I felt like all the air had just been sucked out of me. We couldn't do this without Baxter. I was desperate and he knew it.

"OK, I'll give you one last chance," I told him, generously. "But if you mess up this time…" I let the sentence trail off, not knowing what threat would possibly make any impression on Baxter.

"Yeah, yeah," he said, putting away his whittling. "So…here's what we're gonna do."

Baxter had it all worked out. We just needed eggs and milk. They had plenty of those at the farm. *Someone* would have to go round and ask, possibly beg, maybe even *grovel*. I didn't even bother to ask who that someone might be.

"It's for the team, Bluey," Baxter said, patting me on the back, like I was sacrificing myself for a good cause. And that's just what it felt like.

I was hoping I'd see Dingdong's dad. Dingdong says he likes me because he thinks I'm a nice, polite boy. She always sticks a finger down her throat to let me know she doesn't share his opinion.

But I was out of luck, I found Dingdong and Horseface instead. They had everything ready: a folding table, baskets and boxes of cupcakes, professional-looking signs, tablecloths. They looked like they were organising a street party.

Dingdong thought I'd come to collect them. "We're all ready," she said, cheerfully.

"We're not *quite*," I said. "Just a couple of last minute bits. This and that, you know…" I added vaguely.

"Well, we'll be starting on time," Dingdong told me firmly. "So see you in the park, then." The girls dismissed me with a smile.

"The thing is," I finally blurted out, "we need some eggs…and some milk."

"Don't you think you've left it a bit late?" Dingdong asked, looking at her watch.

"*Los-ers*," Horseface said, smirking.

I ignored her and said to Dingdong, "It's just… we've got no money left."

"Boo hoo, what a shame," Horseface said, sarcastically. "And you want us to help you? This is supposed to be a competition."

She turned to Dingdong. "I can't decide who's the Bigger Loser, him – or Baxter the Brainless."

As badly as we needed those eggs, if I'd had

them in my hands just then, I'd have broken the lot over her head. It was hard enough having to grovel to Dingdong. At least she was one of us. I would never forgive Baxter for making me do this in front of Horseface.

I turned to go, trying to think of something evil enough to say before I walked away empty-handed. But Dingdong saved me the trouble.

"Don't be horrible, Nigella," she said. "It's only a game, for goodness sake. Come on, Banksy, I'll get you the stuff."

I breathed a deep sigh of relief. Dingdong had saved us. As we walked back, I said "Thanks for this. But I'm warning you, it won't stop us trying to beat you."

Dingdong grinned at me. "Obviously. And I'm warning you I've already made a list of jobs for you tomorrow – when you're my slave for the day."

"Keep dreaming," I said, grinning back at her.

I walked past Horseface without even looking at her. I couldn't imagine a worse fate than having her tell me what to do for a whole minute, never mind a whole day. Nothing, not even sitting in a bath full of tarantulas, could come close to that.

Whatever Baxter was planning, we had to go on that park and sell as if our lives depended on it. Because they very nearly did.

CHAPTER SEVEN

Rule Number One, when you're trying to sell something: *first grab your audience.* No point having a great product if there's no one to sell it to. Getting the best pitch to draw the crowds in was our top priority. But guess what: by the time we arrived at the park the girls had already bagged it.

They had the perfect spot: under a big shady tree, with the boating lake behind them, at the top end of the park where the parkie hardly ever comes.

"Those jammy devils," Baxter said.

But the girls weren't jammy; they were organised, like we should have been. They even had a big professional-looking sign that said: *Crazy for Cupcakes.*

"They're crazy," Baxter scoffed. "Stark staring bonkers if they think they're going to win."

But the joke fell as flat as Baxter's over-baked cakes, when we saw the rest of the girls' set-up. They had a proper table, with a big flowery cloth on it. It was covered with plates of cupcakes piled high. They looked ready for business.

"Come on," I said, "let's get our show on the road."

We quickly picked the second best spot, under the nearest tree. It didn't give half the shade the girls had. But we needed to stay close, to keep our eye on them.

Sam and me unpacked all our gear. We tried to keep Glenda the Defender out of it, while Baxter set up the stove and his worktop. I didn't envy him having to do the cooking; it was probably the hottest day of the summer so far.

I was watching the girls and wondering why they hadn't started yet. Everything *looked* ready. They suddenly disappeared, behind the tree.

"They're up to something," I said. "Sam, go find out what."

Sam ran over, followed by the dog, barking and

yapping and giving the game away.

When Sam returned he said, "They've got *balloons*, Banksy. Loads of 'em."

Balloons, why hadn't I thought of that?

"You can't eat balloons," Baxter said, unimpressed. "Wait till people get a whiff of my pancakes cooking. We'll be beating the crowds back with a…*balloon whisk*," he said, grabbing one and waving it around. It wasn't much of a joke but it amused Baxter.

The girls came over then to see what we were up to. We couldn't exactly complain, having sent Sam to spy on them.

Horseface looked at Baxter with the camping stove in front of him. "That won't be allowed," she said, pointing her finger.

"Why not?" I asked. "The only rule we agreed was that we'd make things and sell them."

"And I'm making *pancakes*," Baxter said. "No

rule against that."

"I doubt very much whether the park-keeper would agree," Horseface said. She looked round for him, hoping to grass us up there and then. In school or out, Nigella Horseforth is a five-star snitch.

"Why does it matter what they make?" said Dingdong. "They're not going to beat us."

"But cooking in the park isn't *allowed*," Horseface insisted.

"Selling probably isn't, either," Dingdong pointed out. "But, let's get on with it. And remember, we've still got our *secret weapons*."

Secret weapons? The girls already had all the advantages. I wondered what they were going to throw at us next.

They ducked down behind their stall, then reappeared wearing these *massive* hats they'd made. They were covered with pretend cupcakes.

Leaving Nigella behind the stall, Dingdong walked out into the park with a handful of balloons, calling out, "Cupcakes! Yummy cupcakes!

Free balloon with every cupcake!"

Baxter watched Dingdong and sneered, "You wouldn't catch me making a twit of myself in a daft hat like that. What a pair of idiots."

But I wasn't noticing the daft hats; I was watching the crowds streaming over to the girls' stall.

We're doomed, I thought. Dead in the water.

But that's exactly when you've got to come out fighting: when you think the competition's got you licked. We had to get those crowds away from the girls' stall and over to ours. But how?

Baxter was only just mixing his first lot of batter. "We need something to sell, *now*," I muttered.

"We've still got Baxter's cakes," Sam reminded me.

The little genius had thought to bring them with him. And maybe Baxter was right, covered with icing no one would notice they were burnt to a crisp.

"Quick," I told Sam. We took a box each and I shouted, even louder than Dingdong, "De-licious cake! A penny a slice!"

"*A penny*? That's like giving it away, Banksy?" Sam said.

"It's what the supermarkets do," I explained. "It's just to get people through the door. Once they're inside they *always* buy something else. You watch."

It worked and do you know why? People love to think they're getting something for nothing – or next to nothing.

That's another important business tip: *you can sell anything, if the price is right* – even Baxter's burnt cake.

To be honest, it wasn't as bad as it looked. If you like dead crunchy stuff – that tastes a bit burnt – covered with sugar. Lots of kids did and once we'd got them there, they hung around for the show.

And the one thing we could rely on Baxter for was a good show! He'd given himself a big curly black felt pen moustache that covered half his face. He'd turned a large sheet of paper into a tall chef's hat. And with his mum's apron on he suddenly turned into this over-the-top French TV chef called: *Mon-sewer Pi-erre.* "Allo, allo," he said, grinning.

I don't know how he'd had the nerve to rubbish the girls for looking stupid. Let's face it, looking – *and sounding* – stupid is something Baxter's never been afraid of.

"Ze zecret of ze perrrfect pancake," he began, "or should I zay *c-rrrepe,* iz in ze batte-rrr."

"Is he really going to talk like that?" Sam said, bright red with embarrassment.

"Looks like it," I said grinning.

I couldn't have done it to save my life. But, luckily for us, Baxter hasn't got an embarrassed bone in his body.

He was going to beat the girls at their own game, if it was the last thing he did. Baxter's Big Fat Pancake Show was about to start.

CHAPTER 8

When Baxter said he was going to make pancakes, I admit, I thought, this is a recipe for disaster. I'd tried to argue him out of it – all the way to the park.

"Do you even know how to make them?" I asked.

"A bit of batter and a toss in the pan – how hard can that be?" he said. "The important thing is: it's full of action – *and drama*! People'll pay good money to watch that."

"What people?" I said, still unconvinced.

"All them people who watch cookery programmes on TV. D'you think any of them care about cooking? It's about who's got the best act. It's Britain's Got Talent – *but in the kitchen.* Watch and learn, Banksy," he told me, "watch and learn."

Once the show got started it looked like Baxter was right. He even managed to turn breaking eggs into a performance. He insisted on doing it one-handed – on the edge of the bowl. Even when he missed a couple of times it didn't

bother him. He kept right on until he'd *cracked* it – like a proper chef. Then there was *whisking* – another of *iz special zecrets.* He made that look like an Olympic event. He whisked the batter so violently it was like a tsunami threatening to overflow the bowl. And, Baxter being Baxter, in the end that's what it did. It ran down the front of his apron forming a pool on the tabletop. But Baxter didn't miss a beat. He scooped it back in the bowl and went right on with his patter.

"Ze zecret of a truly *grrreat* pancake," he informed us, "iz 'aving a *verrry* 'ot pan…"

Baxter swirled some butter round the pan and poured in a dollop of mixture. He loosened the edge with a plastic slice.

"And-a now," he said, suddenly going all italian, "for-a my spec-ial party piece: Tozzing ze pancake."

"This'll be a disaster," I heard Dingdong tell

Horseface. With no customers of their own the girls had joined our crowd.

I was worried she might be right. I'd have settled for the cheat's way, flicking it over with a fish slice. But this was Baxter's show and *tozzing* was the main attraction.

For the next few minutes I could hardly bear to watch Baxter half miss and completely miss catching pancakes. The one or two that fell to the ground were snatched up by Glenda the Defender. People were clapping as if she was part of the act.

"Don't worry, zere eez a bit of a knack," Baxter told everyone. "It may need a bit-a more-a *wellie*."

The next time he gave it so *much* wellie the pancake flew up in the air. Baxter held the pan out hopefully, but the pancake never came down. When we all looked up we saw it caught on a low branch immediately above Baxter's head.

Everyone clapped and cheered even harder.

"Great goal, Baxter," someone called out.

Baxter shrugged and grinned, then started off a new pancake. The same thing happened. And a third time! I'll bet you couldn't do that three times in a row if you were trying. Everyone thought it was part of the act. If we'd been charging for the show we'd have made a packet.

But, finally, Baxter got in the swing of it, literally. He was flipping those pancakes and catching them in the pan like a circus performer.

"And-a now, ze final tezzt," Baxter said, handing out the first pancake. Or at least the first that hadn't been on the floor, up a tree, or devoured by the dog.

And to my amazement the verdict was: *not bad*! Soon we were selling pancakes faster than Baxter could make them.

Luckily, yours truly had thought to bring paper plates or people would have been eating them out of their hands. There was jam, or syrup and lemon, or a few other weird toppings on offer: pickled onions (don't even ask!)

Baxter was so hot he was almost steaming. He looked like a ripe tomato by now. He'd gradually stripped off his clothes until he only had a pair of shorts behind his mum's apron. After twenty minutes he took a well-deserved break.

"So what did you think?" he asked us, eagerly.

"Not bad, Baxter," Sam said, scoffing one he'd

poked out of the tree with a long stick.

"I'm not talking about the pancakes," he said, dismissively. "What about the performance?"

"You aced it, Dude," I told him, honestly, and high-fived his sweaty, sticky hand.

The girls were back at their stall, frantically lowering their prices. But as soon as Baxter started cooking again, all their customers drifted back to us.

Later when I looked over the girls seemed to be having a big row. I watched Nigella storm off across the park. Just like her to bale out when it looks like they're losing, I thought. I felt a bit sorry for Dingdong – but only a bit. There was no way I was letting her off being my slave!

"Ready to give in and admit we've won?" I said a few minutes later when she came over.

But that wasn't what Dingdong had come for. "Nigella's gone to find the park-keeper," she warned me. "I tried to stop her, honest. But she says there's no way she's losing, *even if it means playing dirty.*"

So much for Baxter's theory that only boys play dirty, I thought.

I could see Nigella, disappearing across the park. I sent Sam to follow her. "If she finds the park-keeper make sure you get back in time to tip us off."

I thanked Dingdong for warning us.

She shrugged. "I don't want to be *anybody's* slave," she said, through gritted teeth, "but I *hate* snitches."

We stood together watching Baxter, whose act was getting wilder by the minute. He'd started to use the dog to get even more applause. He was tossing the pancakes just out of her reach. Glenda the Defender was barking and bouncing around on two legs just like a circus dog. She was leaping

at exactly the right moments, as if they'd been rehearsing the act for weeks.

Eeryone was clapping and cheering, including Dingdong and me.

"This is going to end in tears," she muttered.

And once again I had a feeling that Dingdong would turn out to be right.

CHAPTER 9

I think I may have told you before that Baxter *always* goes too far. Watching him now with Glenda the Defender, it was clearly an accident waiting to happen.

And it was entirely Baxter's fault. If he hadn't been winding the dog up she might not have leapt at him – and knocked the frying pan out of his hand. Then Baxter might not have lost his balance, and perhaps his hat wouldn't have fallen – right onto the camping stove!

Trying to save the flaming hat, Baxter managed

to knock it over. The camping stove fell sideways, sliding off the tabletop into the bogie, where it set a load of other things alight: the rest of the paper plates, bits of cardboard and packaging and Baxter's old, but much-loved, Disneyworld T-shirt.

Soon a full-blown fire had broken out. It was at that exact moment I heard my name called: "Banksy!!!"

I turned to see Sam running towards us. Less than a hundred metres behind him I could see Horseface – and the park-keeper – legging it in our direction.

If he'd found us just cooking pancakes it would have been bad enough. But in charge of a full-scale bonfire, this was serious stuff that called for desperate action.

"Come on," I told Dingdong, "to the lake."

She knew exactly what to do. We both grabbed hold of the rope that was tied to the front of the bogie and ran as fast as we could, dragging it towards the water. By the time we got there we'd built up quite a bit of speed.

"*Now!!!*" I said to Dingdong.

When we let go of the rope the burning bogie hurtled into the water. It cleared the lake in seconds. Ducks, geese and small water birds took to the air in fright.

Everyone had followed us, so there was quite a crowd to see the dramatic climax of Baxter's Big Fat Pancake Show.

"People won't forget this in a hurry," he breathed.

And he was right.

We all watched the bogie float briefly before it sank into the water. My brilliant plan was working. The water was soon extinguishing the flames. But that wasn't the end of our problems.

Because the lake was so shallow the bogie only sank to the top of its wheels. The evidence sat there in full view, just waiting for the park-keeper. As it smoked in the sunshine the *Bogie of Doom* once again seemed to be living up to its name.

"Quick, get that apron off," I told Baxter. I threw it after the bogie into the water.

The crowd was mainly all kids now, hanging around to watch our fate. By the time the park-keeper reached us Baxter and me had melted into the middle.

"You can't have fires in a public park! It's against the rules," the park-keeper panted, almost completely out of breath.

"I already told them that," Horseface said, smugly.

"Come on, then," he said, ignoring her. "Who's responsible?"

No one spoke. In fact everyone looked around as if they were waiting to see who else might own up.

"Who was it? Who did it? I demand to know!" he said, angrily.

But no one was telling. Horseface couldn't believe we might get away with it. She waved her finger at Baxter. "It was him!" she shrieked. "He did it! He's the one!"

I couldn't understand why she'd singled out Baxter. She really did have a thing about him. But

Baxter kept his cool, looking over his shoulder as if she must mean someone else.

"Was it him?" the park-keeper asked everyone in the crowd. We all copied Baxter's shrug exactly, as if we'd been practising. Still no one said a word.

The park-keeper was getting more and more angry. He whipped a notebook out of his pocket.

"Let's have your name, lad," he said to Baxter.

"William," said Baxter, then helpfully spelled it out: "W-I-double L…"

"Yes, I know how to spell William," the park-keeper snapped.

"Alexander," Baxter went on: "A-L-E-X…"

"He's lying," Horseface shrieked. "His name's Baxter: B-A-X…"

"I can spell Baxter, thank you," the park-keeper cut her off. "Address?" he demanded.

Before Baxter could open his mouth, Horseface had given the park-keeper his full address.

"Your parents will be hearing from me," the park-keeper told Baxter. "And I want that *object* removed, now." He pointed to the half-submerged bogie. "Otherwise I shall add illegal dumping to your other serious offences of arson and vandalism." Then he turned and walked away.

Everyone stared at Nigella Horseforth. Most people already knew her from school. She started to go red.

"You've done some pretty mean things,

Nigella," Dingdong told her through gritted teeth, "but that was by far the meanest."

"I wasn't going to let those *boys* win," she said, as if *boys* was the rudest word in her vocabulary, "even if *you* were."

"I would rather be slave to the boys for a whole day," Dingdong said, "than be your friend for five more minutes."

"As if I care," Horseface said, trying to keep her cool. But her face was getting redder. "It's time I went home anyway," she said, seeing the angry looks she was getting now.

"You'd better," said Baxter, "unless you want to end up on top of the bogie."

"You can't scare me," she said, looking decidedly scared. She turned and half ran across the park. Everyone cheered.

"*Alexander?*" I said to Baxter. "Where'd you get that from?"

Baxter wasn't telling, but Sam was. "It's his middle name."

Baxter gave me a sheepish grin. William *Alexander* Baxter? I learned something new about him every day.

We all looked at the bogie in the lake, then without a word took off our trainers.

"Last one in's a pickled onion," said Dingdong.

We finally dragged it out, covered with duckweed, mud and goose poo. By now, so were we, including Glenda the Defender. The dog smelled *rank* and kept shaking herself all over us.

Dingdong collected all her gear and we piled it on top of ours in the charred remains of the *Bogie of Doom*. We must have looked a pretty sorry sight as we walked home. But Dingdong cheered us up when she opened a last box of leftover cupcakes.

"Hmmm," Baxter told her, "Not bad…for a beginner."

I thought they were *mega de-licious.*

"Have another one," said Dingdong,

generously.

I was just starting to think that *The Get Rich
Quick Club* was finally back on the same side when
Dingdong said, "OK, get your money out, boys.
Let's see who's won?"

CHAPTER TEN

Dingdong opened her purse. "Four pounds twenty-five," she announced. I opened our cash box and counted what little money there was in it. I counted it three times. I checked my pockets; I made Baxter and Sam check theirs. But that was it: three pounds eighty. How had it happened?

"We had far more customers," Baxter argued.

"You must have charged top dollar for those cupcakes," I said.

Dingdong grinned, "We did. But like the advert says: *they were worth it.*"

This was a new lesson in business. When you've got a quality product, you don't need to sell so many to make a good profit. I had to remember that in future.

Baxter looked like he'd been attacked from both sides. He'd been publicly thrown off the park by the park-keeper and now he'd been beaten into submission by girls.

"Don't worry," Dingdong told him, "I'll go easy on you."

"How easy?" I asked.

"You'll find out tomorrow. See you at nine, *slaves*."

Sam went home too. When his mum saw the state of him we could hear her shouts from the shed. Baxter and me sat there, reluctant to go home, imagining the evils Dingdong was planning for us.

"No way am I dressing up," Baxter announced.

"Or dancing the Macarena," I said.

"Or cutting her toenails," Baxter shuddered.

"Or carrying her about," I said, remembering my nightmare. The one crumb of comfort was that Nigella Horseforth wouldn't be involved.

"What if she makes us shave our heads?" Baxter said. He was remembering a boy in our class who came to school one day with a bald head – apart from a fringe. The idiot had done it for a dare.

"I wouldn't do something like that," I said, "not even for money."

"We could go back on it," Baxter suggested.

I knew we could, but it didn't feel right. *A deal's a deal.* That's another of my mottos. No, we'd just have to take our punishment – and take it on the chin.

The next day was a very low day in the history

of *The Get Rich Quick Club*. Dingdong had lied. She wasn't going easy on us for a minute. But the person she brought lowest was Baxter.

Sam spent the entire day spring-cleaning her rat's nest of a bedroom. It's hard to believe, I know, but Dingdong's the scruffiest of all of us. "I'd rather muck out a hundred animal cages than clean up after Miss Piggy again," Sam said.

My job was to wait on her like a...slave.

"Get me this...find me that..." she ordered, all day. Every half hour I had to move her chair into the shade, with her still on it!

She made me cycle up and down to the shop, time after time, in the heat, to get her a snack. And each time I got back she'd changed her mind.

"But you *said*, cheese and onion," I shouted, hot and sweaty.

"I know," she said, sweetly, "but can't a girl

change her mind? I'm in more of a…salt and vinegar mood now."

Baxter was kept busy bringing her drinks all day. Then holding her book out for her while she read.

"My arms get so tired!" she whined. "A bit higher, please."

But Dingdong was saving the best for last. It was ten minutes to five, when our ordeal would finally be over. We were all outside the shed. She suddenly announced, "I feel in the mood for some music now. Sing to me, Baxter," she ordered, handing him a piece of paper with words written on.

She'd brought a camera! "But put these on first," she said passing him a carrier bag. Baxter looked inside; he looked at me. I could tell it wasn't good news.

"Just do it," I said. "Ten minutes and it'll all be a bad memory."

That might have been true for Baxter, but for the rest of us it will always be one of our best memories – *ever*!

It probably sounds cruel to you, laughing at your best mate. But if you'd been there...

Seeing Baxter in one of Dingdong's dance outfits, with a big bow on his head, singing *I'm a Barbie girl, in a Barbie world*...I thought I'd died

and gone to heaven. And Dingdong's got it saved – on video.

It was a brilliant trick, but she had signed her own death warrant.

"Be in no doubt," Baxter promised, "I will get my revenge."

And don't worry, one day he will.

It was almost the end of the holidays. No more business opportunities for a while. I was feeling pretty disappointed with our results.

But then, on Saturday morning, I raced into the shed, so excited I could hardly speak. I was waving around a letter that had just arrived – from the crisp company!

"*We apologise for the unfortunate experience,*" I read aloud from the letter...

"What unfortunate experience?" Baxter demanded.

"The tooth, of course. In the crisp packet. You didn't think I was going to miss that opportunity, did you? Try and keep up, Baxter." I read on, "*And, as an act of good faith, we're sending you compensation!* "

"How much?" Baxter asked, impressed.

I turned over the paper but that was it. "It doesn't say," I shrugged.

We all made guesses: anything between a fiver and £1000 (that was mine, of course). We spent the rest of the morning trying to decide what we would spend it on. I didn't think much of the others' ideas, I can tell you.

Then I got a call on my mobile. It was Mum to say someone had just made a delivery – *for me* – from the crisp company.

We all raced round. I was expecting a letter with a big fat cheque in it. Instead, stacked inside our front door were six big boxes of assorted flavoured *crisps*.

Everyone thought it was the biggest joke.

"Don't spend it all at once, Banksy," Dingdong laughed.

"Watch you don't break your tooth on them," Baxter laughed the loudest. But I didn't care.

You see, that's the big difference between me and him: realistic goals.

I know that Baxter will never wrestle a grizzly bear or catch a crocodile. But one day I *will* be a millionaire.

I'd got six boxes of free crisps. On Monday we'd be back at school. I quickly did a few sums in my head: six boxes, with twenty-five packets in a box…if we sold those at 20p a pack…Oh, yes! We'd be minted.

Move over Lord Sugar, Robin Banks is on his way.